For My Parents

Book One – Tony

"All things truly wicked start from innocence." – Ernest Hemingway

Chapter One

*H*e first started visiting me when I was ten years old. He would come from under the bed in the middle of the night, wearing his black robe, his face always bright white, and his mouth was a black line. At first, I thought he was a figment of my imagination, because his appearance was blurry, like a picture submerged in water. He could have been the boogeyman, the devil, a ghost or a demon. I didn't know what he was or what he wanted.

    I asked him for his true name but he wouldn't say. I asked him if he liked the name "Tony" and he never responded, so I started to call him Tony after his first visit simply because that is the name that came to mind.

    That first time we met was a night in springtime. I remember the heater in the house still kicked on at night but the days were getting warm. I was sound asleep but something woke me up. I heard something under the bed, like a sharp object scraping on the underside of the box spring and against the bed rails. It kept knocking against the bed.

I never needed a night light or the hall lights on because I was never scared, even when I was very little. In the little light that there was, I leaned over the side. I could see the bedspread that hung low on that side had started to bulge. It was slowly expanding, like a balloon blowing up, getting ready to pop. The scraping reached a crescendo as the bulge got bigger and bigger. The bedspread started coming off whatever was causing the bulge.

"Knock it off," I told it. I spoke clearly and in a normal volume. I remember adding profanity to emphasize my irritation with all the noise. I have to admit, I might have cursed at it, but if I admitted that, my mother wouldn't understand. After all, I needed to sleep. I knew profanity was bad, but the noise stopped, so maybe it worked a little. But the moving bedspread kept moving, and that was when Tony presented himself.

Peeking from beneath the covers at me was a face almost translucent in the darkness. He looked at me blankly. Peering over the side of my bed, I looked down at him and he looked up at me.

"I told you to knock it off," I said again. I figured playing it cool would help me figure out if he was real or not. That's when he opened his mouth in an extreme yawn and displayed a disproportionate amount of very sharp teeth. His mouth looked like the mouth of a T-Rex, right out of the movies. My very first thought was, how was anyone supposed to brush all of those teeth? This guy had his own issues.

Tony closed his mouth and looked at me for a moment, like I wasn't reacting the way he wanted me to react, and then he just slinked away, back under the bed.

"Good night, whoever you are. See me in the morning and we'll formally introduce ourselves," I said. I thought, if he was a monster, then I must have been dreaming. He did not respond, at least not verbally. I lay my head back down and drifted off to sleep.

****

3

I woke at the break of dawn. I always had this ability to wake up on time without the alarm clock. The first thing I did was look under the bed. Nothing but my old sneakers, my baseball glove, and a large model of the ship the Cutty Sark my dad gave me for Christmas that I had not put together yet. It did look like something may have been there, because the dust bunnies were moved about, but I couldn't tell for sure.

I was unsure if I had been hallucinating or if Tony may have been part of my 'emotional issues' that Dr. Erkahn told my mother he thought I had. Luckily my mother did not believe in medication or I would have been put on some happy pill. They didn't medicate me, but my parents were convinced I had something wrong with me. I was convinced that I did not. True, I had few friends – if any. Teachers said I was "apathetic towards others" and "showed little emotion." My response to them was that most people bored me and there was nothing much to get excited about. After a few months of nonstop work persuading my father not to send me to counseling sessions, I somehow convinced Dad, who convinced Mom, and I stopped seeing Dr. Erkahn.

My grades were excellent, I was respectful to everyone, I obeyed my parents without much pushing back and I completed all the chores they assigned to me. They were still concerned that while other kids in the neighborhood were out riding bikes and playing cowboy I was reading or drawing or watching monster movies. Comic books and monster movies were what I lived for. Most of the kids in the neighborhood were nice but they were as mentally challenging as counting to five.

My actual 'problem' was that I was tested to have an IQ of about 160, which anyone would admit was rather high. So, at ten years old, I was already in high school. It was a private school so I needed to wear slacks and a collared shirt, and because it was located in the next town, Mom would have to drive me and pick me up there every school day. She always avoided the center of town, making the trip longer, but I think that was her excuse for taking the time to ask me questions about me and my life in the hope I'd open up to her. I actually liked being in high school, not so much for the studies but for the girls. I spent time with some really cute girls and I think they enjoyed my company. I could make them laugh fairly easily even though I never considered myself funny. Their boyfriends and the guys in the class liked me, too. Sure, I helped them with their school work; more importantly, I helped their girlfriends with their homework. Since I was ten, the boys felt that they could trust me with their girlfriends. I dreamt of the beautiful girls. I loved them but, unfortunately, they only *liked* me.

So it was comic books and monster movies unless one of the neighborhood kids got bored and there was no one else around but me. Then we'd hang out, and read comic books and watch monster movies together. I never really had a close friend, until I met Tony. Tony always challenged me, which is what I liked best about him.

✱✱✱✱

Tony came back the next night around the same time. First there was the scraping and then the banging. I was surprised my parents couldn't hear the racket.

"Why do you make so much noise?" I said, barely awake. The noise stopped so I sat up and waited. After a while nothing happened so I lay back down. The noise started again.

"Really, who does that?" I questioned. I think I was really knocking him off of his game because the noise stopped. There was more light that evening and I had left the blinds open. I saw him rise at the foot of the bed; the same white, glowing face and the same shapeless black robe. I don't think Tony had any feet, not that I saw any. He seemed to be floating there, at the end of my bed.

"Hello again," I said. He just stared back looking like a ghost from the Pac Man game.

"Okay, how it works on Earth with normal people is that when the host greets a guest, the guest responds. Do you want to try?" I was getting a little ticked. I didn't need to get up in the middle of the night to someone or something with bad manners. Not a word from Tony, but I began to suspect that he was trying to menacing when what he was really doing was acting like a jerk.

Finally, Tony floated, or walked or whatever he did to get there, to the wall to my left. I didn't hear anything, but his robe reached out and slowly claw marks appeared on the wall. Blood began to drip from the marks in the wall.

"What are you doing? You are a jerk! My Dad will have a fit if he sees that," I snapped. I must have yelled at him, because I heard my mother get out of bed, I heard my parent's bedroom door open. It would only be moments before she came into my room. Tony must have heard it too because he disappeared under the bed. I almost felt like joining him.

My door opened and Mom flicked on the light switch.

"What is going on in here? Are you talking in your sleep?" Mom looked at me with one eye, her other eye still closed, not yet adjusted to the light. I was looking at the wall to inspect the damage but there was nothing there. Tony's handiwork seemed to be self-repairing, which was convenient.

"Hi Mom, I was dreaming." I answered. She considered it for a moment.

"Well, dream a little quieter. OK, kiddo?" Mom said as she kissed my cheek. She tucked my blankets around me tight and shut out the light as she left the room. I waited for him to come back out but Tony took the rest of the night off. After a little while, I finished my eight hours of sleep.

Chapter Two

J had a sleepover at my house when I was eleven. Manny Torres, a kid who lived at the end of my street and was awesome at skateboarding, invited himself over. Manny never made fun of me; he wanted to know more about what it was like in high school, particularly what the girls were like. He liked my house and my parents; and, he especially liked my Dad's car. Manny was actually cool in the eyes of all the other kids, not just me. That was what was so unbelievable about him wanting to stay over; he was a cool kid who liked to hang out with me. Being cool wasn't all that important to me but it was a bonus if a cool kid liked you or, better yet, thought that you were cool as well. It made life a little easier.

At the age of eleven, Manny was already getting dark peach fuzz above his upper lip. He was taller than the rest of the kids our age and his voice had already begun to deepen. Naturally, he was interested in the fairer sex and was eager to voice his opinions on the matter whenever he was able. Manny also had a tough home life so a night at someone else's house was probably an escape for him. I don't know what his father did but he was rarely home; his mother worked part time at the mall and was usually home nights and weekends. His older brother was also in high school and always in some kind of trouble.

Of course, my first thoughts were of my other friend, Tony, who was becoming a burden, especially at times like these. I was concerned that Tony would make his appearance the night of the sleepover and Manny would go running out of the house into the night, screaming his head off. I'd always be known as the "spooky kid" after that and lose the few friends I had. Of course, I knew I already was the "spooky kid" but no one else needed to know that.

My plan was for us to sleep in the living room if my parents were OK with it. I'd lay out the sleeping bags and pillows then we could watch some monster or science fiction movie and eat popcorn. I liked the idea of being like the other more "normal" kids.

The night of the sleep over came and we did get to sleep in the living room. Mom and Dad stayed for a little while but they had a TV in their room so they retired early. We did have popcorn and sneaked some other treats as well. We watched *Creature from the Black Lagoon* and went to sleep after it ended. It was a pretty pleasant evening.

At about two in the morning, there was a sound coming from the basement of the house. Then I heard footsteps, something was slowly climbing upstairs. As always, I was a light sleeper so I awoke and sat up. Manny rolled over as well. He wasn't quite awake but his eyes were slightly open. I had left the bathroom light on so that Manny could find his way if he woke up in the middle of the night.

I could see the handle on the cellar door move back and forth slightly then began to turn more fully. The door creaked open as perfectly as it would in an old, scary movie. Out pops Tony the scary monster dressed in his best black cloak. Actually, it was the same black cloak and luminescent face that he always wore. I never had seen Tony in a different room of the house and, at first, was a bit confused by his appearance at the cellar door. Manny stared at Tony not saying a word. Then I became really angry at him.

"Tony. What the heck are you doing out of my room? You get out this instant!" I said in a loud whisper. "I said go! Now! I'll have a word with you later, mister."

Tony lingered for a moment then turned around. He closed the cellar door as he descended the stairs and latched it quietly. Once the footsteps stopped I turned to Manny; his eyes were only slits. He may or may not have seen Tony but, if he did, he was taking it well. I lay down and went back to sleep.

****

The next morning Manny awoke and told me about a crazy dream he'd had. Something had come up the stairs and opened the door. It was some kind of ghost or monster but I had told it off and it left us alone. Manny was quite impressed with me; maybe Tony wasn't such a burden after all. We had pancakes for breakfast then dressed to go outside. It was a Saturday morning and Manny never stayed in to watch cartoons. He wanted to go shoot hoops at the basketball net on a telephone pole near his house. I was terrible at basketball but went with him anyway. I would catch up on my Warner Brothers some other time.

We began to play Horse, and Manny was at the "S" before I got my "H" even though, I suspected, he was not trying as hard as he usually did. His brother's Mustang was in the driveway and Manny admired it as much as he admired his brother. When his brother came out of the house he joined us at the basketball net. We played a little two on one and actually beat him. While we were playing, Manny retold his dream to his brother who told me I was a "tough guy" for getting rid of the monster for Manny. I guess Manny had bad dreams often; at least that's how his brother made it sound.

After that sleepover, I was more accepted by the kids in the neighborhood. They still poked fun at me for being a "dork" or a "nerd" but it was more lighthearted and playful than it had been. Some kids could be menacing, even downright mean. I didn't really care all that much, because I knew that after high school was college then graduate school, and I would be with people more like me. I probably wouldn't run into the neighborhood kids all that often by then.

At that time the neighborhood kids were my peers, for better or worse, so I decided to do what I could to be accepted or, at least, acceptable to them. I was still apathetic towards them but I viewed my budding friendships as a social experiment. The reality was that, other than a couple of kids, the children of my age group were merely tall babies. They cried and moaned, and made little sense most of the time. It was painful to communicate with them. Manny was an exception; he wasn't the brightest bulb in the house but he had a social skill that put anyone at ease including myself. The other exception I had was a girl named Cadence.

****

Cadence was my first crush; she was everything I thought I wanted. She was tall and beautiful with long, blonde hair. She had big, bright blue eyes and a smile with perfect, white teeth. She was definitely a heartbreaker. I felt connected to her was because she was also a nerd.

Cadence attended the same school and the same grade as the other kids our age but she was in the advanced classes. She loved science and chemistry and she excelled at mathematics. She had read dozens upon dozens of great literary works on her own, often doubling or tripling the required summer reading lists. She was a splendid specimen in every way and I had met her through Manny. She was his girlfriend.

Cadence would help Manny with his math and science homework and they would play billiards when they were done. Manny's dad had a pool table in a playroom he constructed in their cellar. The room had a built in bar and a couch with a television high on a shelf so it could be seen from anywhere in the room. When we weren't outside and Manny's father wasn't home, we were in the cellar.

In the beginning, I was horrible at pool but with the use of geometry and physics I began to master it enough to be passable. Manny, like his brother, was a brilliant pool player and could make different trick shots. Cadence liked to play but wasn't completely swept up in the game. We were playing pool not too long after the sleepover when Manny told us of his dream at my house. It seemed that Cadence knew Manny frequently had nightmares so she also was pleased that I somehow brought a happy ending to that one.

I never thought I'd tell them the story of how I met Tony. Manny was telling us that he hadn't had a nightmare since the sleep over and Cadence was asking him for all the details.

"Tell me more about the monster," Cadence asked Manny, while missing a shot.

"He was real tall; he had a black cape and big boots. His face was white and he had long arms with long claws," Manny answered. Stupidly, I corrected him.

"No, Tony doesn't have feet and rarely will he use his arms," I said. Cadence caught on quickly.

"Tony – who is Tony? How would you know what Manny dreamed?" she asked me.

"Oh, I've heard him tell the story a few times," I lied.

Then Manny jumped in. "Yeah, but I never had a name for him. I just said he was scary and had a white face," Manny said to me. I wanted to change the subject quickly so I took my cue and lined up my next shot. It chipped a striped ball and bounced a solid into the corner pocket; I was trying to sink the striper.

"Your turn, Manny," I said. He looked at me for a moment then prepared his next shot.

"Have you ever seen a monster in your nightmares like that?" Manny asked.

"No, I sleep pretty soundly," I replied. Cadence wasn't buying what I was selling.

"I think you have" she said to me. I became defensive and a little flustered.

"No, no, nothing like that. Like I said, I don't have nightmares," I answered back.

"Then who is Tony?" she asked. I was never a good liar. both stopped and looked at me. I sighed and shrugged my shoulders, deciding to tell them and see how they would take it.

"Tony is the monster that lives under my bed. He's the same *thing* that came up the cellar stairs the night you stayed over. I had never seen him in any other room in the house other than my bedroom. That is why I wanted to sleep in the living room in the first place. What you saw, Manny, actually happened."

The way that Manny looked at me made me afraid I was losing my best friend. But the story was out in the open and all I could do was hope for the best.

"You're kidding me" was all that Manny could say. Cadence looked a little taken back by this as well. She stood alongside Manny, as if awaiting my explanation.

"No, I am not. He is real, apparently, as you have seen him. I thought he had been something out of my imagination all these years. I had been the only one to ever see him before you did."

I could see their minds at work by the expression on their faces. I expected a flurry of questions but Cadence surprised us both.

"I need to see him," she said to me.

The logistics involved were a bit staggering. She wanted to be in my house in the middle of the night. This would be the only possible time Tony would be "available." My parents, as well as Cadence's parents, would probably not opt for a boy/girl sleepover. I had an idea, however, this was the only way both Cadence and Manny would meet Tony.

Chapter Three

*M*anny was a little reluctant at first to sleepover again, we both knew it would involve little actual sleep. Manny and I had permission to use the living room again; my parents were happy with the fact I was making real friends in the neighborhood. Cadence lived on a side street about four houses down on the right.

She planned to sneak out of her bedroom after midnight and come over. Since we were in the living room she could alert us that she was there by brushing past the shrubs and tapping on the window quietly. Manny and I would let her in and we would hunker down on the floor and wait for Tony. We planned it for Friday again so that we wouldn't have to get up early for school the next day. I made them both promise to keep this to ourselves.

The following Friday Manny came by for supper; he wasn't as talkative as he had been before. We set up the sleeping bags and the snacks but didn't watch any scary movies — Manny was on edge enough. My folks retired while we watched *Star Trek* reruns; our conversation was spotty and superficial. We waited while the clock and the reruns ticked away the hours until it was almost midnight. We turned off all the lights except the one in the bathroom down the hall. A short time later, there was a tap on the window. Manny jumped.

I opened the window and in came Cadence. After a brief greeting, we simply sat and waited. We situated ourselves so we had a direct line of sight from the living room towards the cellar door in the kitchen. Both Cadence and Manny looked worried; the night had stolen their bravery. Fortunately we did not have to wait long. There was a thud in the cellar. I could tell it was my father's golf clubs dumping onto the floor — Tony was always a bit clumsy. There were footsteps slowly climbing the cellar stairs. The door handle turned.

Manny was pale and breathing fast and heavy; Cadence's eyes were like saucers, they were so big. The door creaked open and out came Tony. His flowing robe touched the floor but he seemed to float. He left the door open and a cold draft drew the air in the room. Tony came a little closer, and I stood up to introduce him.

"Tony, this is Manny and Cadence. Manny and Cadence, this is Tony," I said formally.

No one spoke or moved. I was sure that Cadence and Manny were scared speechless so I tried to pry them.

"Tony doesn't bite. He really doesn't do anything. He's a good listener though."

Manny finally spoke up, "What is he?"

"I'm not sure but I guess he's real if you two are seeing him," I said.

"He's a real apparition," Cadence added in a voice just above a whisper.

"Yeah, but he's pretty useless. He's been haunting me for a couple of years or so now, he doesn't do much except annoy me," I explained.

"Have you tried to communicate with him?" Cadence asked.

"Sure, I've talked to him, written him notes, I even tried other languages but he doesn't say anything," I said.

"Does he do anything other than just...I dunno...float there?" Manny asked.

"Once in a while he scratches things but the marks fade away, sort of like disappearing ink. I've seen his teeth a couple of times but I think that's when I've ticked him off."

"He has teeth?" Manny said "I can barely see his mouth."

"Oh yeah, teeth that would make a shark jealous; tons of them that are long and pointy, not in a row, kind of all over the place."

"Make him go away now, please," Cadence said softly. I knew she had had enough of Tony already.

"OK Cadence. Tony, Cadence says it's time for you to go home – or wherever you go when you leave here. Take tomorrow night off, I'll see you the next day," I said, and after a moment, he slowly backed his way towards the cellar door. Tony had always been obedient and I never considered he would act otherwise. As he glided down the stairs, the cellar door closed and quietly latched itself shut. I turned to Manny and Cadence with an air of pride. It was as if I had shown them my new bicycle or something.

Manny and Cadence rose in unison; the sleepover had ended. Manny looked like he wouldn't be able to sleep for several days after what he just saw, Cadence too.

"I'll walk Cadence home. I'm going home after that. Sorry, I can't stay here tonight after all of this," Manny said.

I didn't mind either way. I led them to the front door and let them out. They left without another word. I left the mess in the living room for the morning and retired to my bedroom for a good night's sleep.

****

I saw both Manny and Cadence the next afternoon; they had bags under their eyes. They had to come by to see me and convince themselves that what they saw was real. We sat outside on the front porch as they declined my invitation into the house. I assured them again that what they'd seen was real.

"You really met Tony. It really happened," I said.

"Why is his name Tony? Did he tell you his name?" Cadence asked.

"No, I gave it to him when he first started coming around. I didn't know what to call him and I wanted to see what he'd do. But he didn't do anything, which I found out was usual for him. He never does," I said.

"Do you think he's dangerous?" Manny asked. I had considered this more lately, seeing how he was not a figment of my imagination after all.

"Nah, I don't think he's here to hurt anyone," I said with as much confidence as I could.

The conversation faded but no one made a move to leave, they were lost in their own thoughts. At least they felt safer in the day light; safe enough to come in the yard anyway. A Mustang drove down the street heading home and it slowed as it passed our house. Manny's brother put the car in neutral and revved the engine for us. He gave a quick wave and was gone. Manny took it as his cue to leave and he got up, said his goodbyes and began to walk home. Cadence stayed put; something was on her mind.

"What's it like to be a sophomore?" she asked me.

"It's fine. You have a question about high school?" I said.

"No, just making conversation," she replied.

"Why don't you say what's really on your mind, Cadence?" I looked at her surprised that I was sounding more like my father.

"That thing that lives in your house; what do your parents think about it?"

"They don't know about Tony; they've never seen him. I'm still not sure that he can be seen or wants to be seen by adults. I'll have to try that, though," I said as I stood up.

"Try what?" Cadence said looking up at me.

"I'm going to try to get my parents to meet Tony."

Chapter Four

$\mathcal{B}$y Sunday night, I had already done my homework and completed a book report that was not due for another week. I started preparing my science experiment for the science fair even though it was many weeks away. I was considering cloning as a topic but was unsure how I could pull that off.

My most compelling project was Tony and how to get my parents to see him. I started with a phone call to my grandmother. For the past thirty years or so my grandmother had been filming the family's annual activities. Birthdays and Christmases and Easters, all were caught on 8-millimeter movie film.

She had had them developed and put on a big reel and once a year, usually on Thanksgiving, we would watch her compilation of holidays throughout the years. The adults would drink and get sentimental, laughing over something they did years ago or crying over a family member they saw on the screen that was no longer among us. For a while, it was interesting seeing the different clothing styles and automobiles in the driveway. The earlier films were in black and white and the later ones were in color. I liked to run the projector and Grandma was happy to let me.

Then Grandma bought a video camera. After I begged, she let me use it last Christmas. It was about twelve pounds and came with a tripod that mounted to a threaded hole on the bottom, but I preferred to have it sit on my shoulder just like I was a camera man for the evening news. It had two rechargeable batteries and it took a VHS tape. It had a little red light that came on when the record button was activated. Once filming was done, we could pop it into the video player and watch, no more developing. I was calling Grandma because I knew I needed the camera to catch Tony on film, or video.

Grandma was careful about her things and kept them in nice condition so it proved a little difficult at first to get her to release the camera to me. It was a couple of years old but it was still her baby. When she asked what I wanted it for I told her I had an interest in filmmaking. She said she felt that if I had a hobby then it would benefit me in the long run. I promised to take care of it. So that Monday, after school, Mom drove me over to Grandma's to pick it up.

I set the camera up in my room on the tripod. I had to push my bureau to make room for it and get the angle facing the foot of the bed and the closet. It was easy to set up and it even came with a small but bright spotlight that mounted on top of the camera. The light used an electrical cord so I had to cobble together a few extension cords to give the camera freedom of movement. Once that was done, I shut off the lights and tried to sleep for a while.

That night, Tony was early. His banging woke me up around 1 am. He was coming out from under the bed so I quickly activated the video camera and the light on top. I nearly blinded myself. I might as well have used a search light it was so bright. Tony made a guttural noise and the banging stopped. It was unusual to hear Tony at all but he definitely grunted in some way. My eyes adjusted and I aimed the camera in his general direction. The camera was set for wide angle as I was not in position to look through the lens.

"Tony," I stage whispered, "Tony, are you there?" Tony disappeared under the bed and did not return that evening. I had spooked him. I went to the camera and stood where I could look in the lens. The camera could replay what was just taped through the view finder but it would not have sound. There wasn't much tape as the visit was so short. I rewound the tape and pressed "play."

The video was briefly dark then there was a blinding light. Even the camera needed a moment to adjust itself. For a brief moment I could see part of Tony's own shadow on the wall. The light cast the shadow up the wall towards the ceiling but Tony was gone in an instant. All you could see was the end of the bed and the closet with its doors pulled shut. The camera never captured his face.

I was still confident that something had to be on the videotape. The visual left much to be desired but I knew there was still the audio to investigate. I pressed "eject" and took the tape downstairs to the television in the living room. I popped it into the VCR, and made sure the volume was down low. I pushed the tape into the player and pressed "Rewind." In seconds it was done, so I pressed "Play."

I saw the same darkness but now I could hear Tony's banging. It sounded distant and dull. Then there was the bright light that quickly faded and brought the room into view. As the light faded I saw the shadow again on the wall but it disappeared so quickly. It looked like the figure of a man but then again it could have been something else. The audio was terrible; the camera had picked up all the local noises closest to the microphone. There was the thud of me turning on the light and my hand adjusting the camera. It sounded like I was in an earthquake.

In the background, though barely audible, was a groan. It was low and very short, a sound that I couldn't recreate vocally. I had captured Tony on videotape, if even for a moment. I realized that the recording I made was worthless to anyone else. It basically showed a kid turning on the camera in his darkened bedroom really quickly and not much more. At least I knew it was possible for Tony to be captured on tape. I went back to bed somewhat deflated.

****

Morning came and I checked under my bed and in the closet like I did every day. I also began to patrol the cellar as well. I never found anything of interest but I needed to be sure. I dressed and went downstairs. Mom was up and greeted me with breakfast.

"How did the movie making go?" she asked.

"Oh, pretty good. Just getting the hang of using the equipment," I said as I stuffed frosted flakes into my mouth.

"What are you filming in your room?"

"Not much, yet." I hoped she would drop it.

"Well, don't damage anything or your Grandma will be very upset. Make sure that stuff is ready to go back to her this weekend."

"I will."

"I'll be ready to take you to school in 10 minutes. Make sure you brush your teeth." She kissed my head as she walked out of the kitchen. I still had a couple more days with the camera so I could try again. If I could get Tony on tape I'd really have something to show them.

Chapter Five

$\mathcal{T}$ony rarely visited several nights in a row. More often if he came one night, chances were he would not come the next. But just in case, the next night, I had the camera set-up in my room at the ready.

I wondered if Tony was camera shy. I wasn't even sure if Tony knew what a camera was. I guessed it was more likely the bright light that scared him off. Tony's visits were always when available light was at a premium.

After school Mom picked me up as usual in her aging Volvo station wagon. She liked the car even though the miles were piling up; Dad liked it because it was paid for. He drove a more recent Lincoln, which was loaded with leather and power everything. If we went out as a family, we would take the Lincoln. I preferred the Volvo because it was quiet, but other than that, all I cared about cars was that they worked.

When we pulled into our driveway, Cadence was there waiting for me. She wore her Levis and had her hair in a ponytail; I was in my standard issue khakis and collared shirt. She had ridden her bike over; she looked worried about something because she was twirling her hair again, and I remembered she'd done that twirling the night she met Tony. Mom went into the house leaving me to talk to my friend in private. Most likely she watched from the kitchen.

"Hi Cadence, what's new?" I asked.

"Hopefully nothing much more exciting than the other night," she said a little nervously. She paused and I waited for her to continue. I could tell she had something on her mind so I gave her time to put the words together. "Manny's having some trouble."

"What kind of trouble?"

"He's really freaked out about your friend, Tony."

I was actually surprised by this, as Tony was so confident and smooth, especially for a kid our age. I waited for Cadence to explain, but she didn't. So I had to pull the information from her. "Why is he so freaked out?"

"You know he's always had night terrors, didn't you? Tony's kind of pushed them to the next level," she said.

"How?"

"I just came from there. He hasn't gone to school, so I went to see if he was

okay. Even his older brother is worried about him. He's scared. That's it. He's just so afraid."

"I didn't know Manny was so sick, but what can we do?" I asked. I really was at a loss.

"I don't know; that's why I came to you. You're so smart; you'll think of something," she said almost pleadingly.

"Manny's folks are going to have to get him to a doctor, an analyst of some kind. I never knew Manny suffered from emotional issues. If I did, I probably wouldn't have had him meet Tony," I said. I took her hand, and she didn't pull away. Ever since I met her, I had wanted to do that. I held it for some time, until she spoke.

"You should go talk to him" Cadence said to me, pulling her hand away.

"Seeing me is the last thing he needs, Cadence, really. If you're close to his parents, maybe you should tell them he needs to see a therapist or something."

"You really think he needs counseling?" It was more a statement than a question.

"Yes, and it's up to his family to help him."

"I still think you should talk to him." She was still unsure of herself.

"I don't know what good that will do, but if he's willing to talk to me." I finally gave in.

Her eyes smiled. She had gotten what she wanted and mounted her bicycle to go.

"I'll find out and let you know. Thanks," She said and peddled off down the street. I saw her turn onto her side street and knew she was going home. I went into the house wondering how I could help my friend Manny with his mental health issues.

****

My homework was done, my teeth were brushed and I was in bed by 9:30. The camera equipment had already been checked and was ready. It took a little longer than usual to fall asleep but once there I was gone to the world. I never remembered my dreams. I wondered if I dreamed at all. Sleeping was, and is, like shutting off a light switch. The next thing I know it's the morning — or a visit from Tony. This time Tony was a no show.

****

With school, a ride home from Mom, and a visit from Cadence, Wednesday was a repeat of Tuesday. The differences were only in the clothes Cadence and I were wearing. She had already been to see Manny, who said he was feeling better. Manny's mother had taken him to his pediatrician that morning, because Manny's night terrors had worsened and he could not sleep. The doctor said that if these terrors persisted, he would recommend a specialist for Manny to see. The doctor gave Manny's mother a prescription for a mild sedative and Manny took a long nap. When Cadence visited him after school, she had woken him. She said he looked better.

Then she said, looking around to be sure my mother had gone into the house, "You were right; he doesn't want to talk to you, at least not yet. He's not mad at you but he's not ready now. Maybe in a couple of days."

"No problem, I can wait. Tell him I hope he feels better soon," I said, genuinely wishing for Manny's recovery. My apathy towards others had apparently started to waver.

"He'll feel better when Tony's gone, so will I. Is there something you can do to get Tony to leave?" she whispered, afraid Tony would hear her.

"I've never clicked my heals three times and wished him away if that's what you're asking."

"Be serious! I think he's scary, and maybe even dangerous. We're afraid he'll come to our houses next," Cadence said.

I had never thought of that. Even though Tony had shown no signs of going anywhere, he was not consistent. Then she asked, "Have your parents seen him yet?"

"No, not yet. I borrowed my Grandma's video camera and I'm trying to get Tony on tape so I can show them," I told her. Then without thinking, I said, "I think that if parents or any grown up sees him he will leave."

"Oh, I hope so. Please try," Cadence said.

"I have been but I've got nothing so far. He didn't come last night, so he'll probably be around either tonight or tomorrow. I have to give the camera back this weekend so those are my last chances to record him, at least for now."

Cadence handed me a small piece of folded paper, it had doodles and her phone number on it; she obviously wrote it in school and held onto it until she had seen me. "Call me if you need to," she told me. She kissed my cheek, mounted her bike and left. I stood there for a moment not sure what to do. I just watched her peddle away, turning onto her own street.

Mom greeted me in the kitchen with a knowing smile. She tussled my hair as I passed by then went back to preparing dinner while I went to my room.

****

Before bed, Mom came in to say goodnight. I had said goodnight to Dad downstairs while he was watching television. I could tell that Mom wanted to ask about Cadence; I wanted to get some sleep before Tony arrived.

"I like your friends; I hope you see more of them," Mom said. I knew Mom was happy to see me socializing.

"Cadence is alright. She's pretty smart, too," I parried with her. I had Mom figured out a long time ago and knew what to expect.

"Not to mention – she's a cutie," Mom said.

"Yes, I guess so," This was all I could say though I agreed with her more than I was willing to show. It was time to change gears and lay the groundwork for telling both my parents about Tony.

"I have other friends, Mom."

"I like Manny, too."

"Yes but there's another; I'd like for you to meet him."

"Well, have him come over. Maybe he can join us for dinner some time."

"I don't know if he'd come for dinner but I guess anything is possible," I said with some hesitation.

"Good night, kiddo." She kissed my cheek and left my room. I was unsure of Tony's diet and wondered if he ate at all. After knowing him for some time, I still had too many questions. I rechecked my gear and got into bed. Sleep came without dreams.

Chapter Six

*B*anging and scratching, banging and scratching — for someone (or something) that didn't talk, Tony sure made a lot of noise. This time I didn't turn on the camera light. I just let the camera record with the light that was in the room. The hallway light was on but it was at the other end of the hall near the bathroom. It cast little my way.

The closet door, a pitch dark square at the other side of an almost dark room, rattled then slowly opened. Tony's glowing face appeared and remained in place long enough for me to take in his brilliance. I was already sitting up to activate the video camera; I waited until Tony entered the room. He didn't disappoint.

Tony floated into the room. I heard his cloak brush against the closet door. I was elated that he provided sound for recording. There was a deep guttural purr from him, like a lion breathing, soft and low. This was turning into one of the most active visits we've ever had. Tony came closer, passing the end of my bed. He glided up the pathway between the bed and the dresser until he was only a few feet away, towering over me.

"What's your problem?" I asked. No answer, of course, just more staring and floating. Slowly his arms came from under his robe, claws extending outward. His left arm reached the dresser and began knocking off what was kept there. My keys, hairbrush, deodorant and glass coin jar crashed to the floor loudly enough for my parents to hear. It shattered on the floor, releasing every coin to clang and roll every which way across the floor. This was something new.

"Hey, what the heck are you doing?" I said too loudly but I didn't care. I was pretty mad at the mess he made. Tony's face suddenly came down to meet mine straight on. I could see that his skin looked like rubber; his eyes were just black holes. I could hear Tony hiss; his mouth was opening to reveal his Tyrannosaurus like teeth.

My parents' door opened.

Tony's advance became a retreat. He was *sucked* under the bed like the air being let from a balloon, gone in an instant. My father was at the door in a white t-shirt and boxers, his hair wild from sleep.

"What is going on in here?" Dad said, turning on the light. I was still sitting up in bed so I stood to see the dresser and the remains of my belongings. Instead of magically reappearing in place as if never touched, the keys, hairbrush, deodorant were on the floor with the carnage of my coin jar. This was the first time Tony had left behind evidence of his visit.

"Son, why did you wake me up? It's 2:30 in the morning, what are you doing?" He asked again.

"Sorry, Dad, I must have knocked it over in the dark by accident," I said to him still looking at the wreckage.

"Were you talking to yourself?" This came out more as a statement instead of a question; Dad was used to my erratic behavior. He sometimes needed to point out my obvious errors if and when I made them.

"Sorry Dad, I'll go back to sleep" was all I could say. He didn't say another word. He turned around and patted back to their bedroom. I heard the door close.

I was taken a bit by surprise by Tony. He rarely got close and he never left any marks or knocked things over; he was usually very tidy. If he ran his claws across something, the marks would be gone by morning. I decided I would wait until morning to clean up.

Then I remembered the video camera. The red light was still on. I had recorded everything including my father's visit. I shut the camera off delicately as if I could accidently press something to make the recording disappear. My shock turned to giddiness as I realized I had a recording of Tony that I could show to whomever. I would first have to view it myself and make sure it captured everything.

After waking up my father, I decided it would not be prudent to turn on the television in the living room. He was a level-headed guy but waking him up twice would definitely piss him off. I would have to wait until morning. I unplugged the camera equipment just on the chance I might activate something and wipe out the recording. I then hopped back into bed and, after a while, drifted off to sleep.

****

Morning came and I was dressed and downstairs early. I wanted to view the tape before my mother got out of the shower. As I turned on the VCR, I felt excited to see what I had captured. It was a brilliant performance; Tony was in rare form. Hopefully the tale of the tape would show me how brilliant the performance was.

The television screen was blue as I slipped in the video tape and pressed "Rewind." The tape made its whirring noise as it sped back to the beginning. It stopped and I pressed "Play." I stood back and watched the screen.

It was dark and grainy. Naturally, the hallway light was all but useless to the camera. I then heard the banging clearly; it was distant but definitely there. I heard my closet door handle unlatch and the door open. I still couldn't see a thing but hoped Tony's luminescence would change that.

I could see the glow in the closet but it was really blurry, like a flashlight far away. Tony floated into the room; I could hear the ruffle of the cloak against the closet door. The light was high in the frame; his face showed no visible features at all. I couldn't see his cloak either and the camera seemed to have been out of focus. I made sure that the camera was on auto focus each night before bed. Could the camera have been unable to focus on Tony for some reason? I hoped I hadn't screwed something up.

I heard Tony's purr, the lion sound. I heard it plain as day. Seconds later I could hear my own voice ask, "What's your problem?" The light hovered in place for a moment; I then heard his claws on the dresser and the items falling to the floor. It was followed by the crash of the coin jar and my voice again asking, "Hey, what the heck are you doing?"

The light grew larger and sunk to the middle of the screen. I heard the hiss followed immediately by the very far away sound of my parents' door opening. The light disappeared as if turned off. I could hear my father's recorded footsteps as I pressed "Stop." I rewound the tape. I wanted to see the end of the visit again.

I stopped the tape from rewinding and pressed "Play." The tape picked up with the light high on the screen. The noise of the falling objects was followed again by my question. The light grew and moved to the center of the screen. I increased the volume on the television so I could actually *hear* Tony. Then came the hiss.

I rewound and played again to hear the hiss; I turned up the volume even louder. The light grew and centered on the screen. Then I heard it.

"YYYYYYYEEEEEEEEESSSSSSSSSSSSSSSSSSSSSSSSSS"

I was really shocked; the hiss sounded like the word "yes." I rewound and played again.

"YYYYYYEEEEEEEEEESSSSSSSSSSSSSSSSSSSSSSSSSS"

It was a word. Tony said the word "Yes" to me; right to my face in fact. Tony could speak.

Chapter Seven

$\mathcal{I}$ turned off the television and VCR just as my mother arrived in the living room. I would need to wait till after school to review the tape more.

"Good morning, mother," I said.

"Good morning sweetie. Watching TV before school?"

"Yeah, just checking the weather."

"What do you want for breakfast?"

"I'll have some cereal."

"Cereal it is," she said and went into the kitchen. With the tape in my hand, I was on the stairs when she called to me, "Did you have a nightmare or something last night?"

I stopped. "No Mom, I just knocked some stuff over. I'm sorry if I woke you up." I heard her taking dishes from the cabinets and the refrigerator door open.

"Your Dad woke up. Not me. I must've slept through the whole thing." I heard her moving about the kitchen, and I continued up the stairs to my room. I hid the tape in my sock drawer, figuring the most obvious place was the last place someone would look, although I was highly skeptical that we would be robbed that particular day.

****

When I got home from school, the first thing I did was go inside the house to my room to check on the tape. It was still there in the drawer. I left my book bag on my bed and headed back downstairs to the kitchen for a snack. Mom had left chicken on the counter to thaw; I grabbed a couple of Oreos and some milk. I leaned against the counter and looked at the packaged chicken. It was a large pack of legs and thighs spread out on a Styrofoam tray covered in clear plastic wrap. The legs and bones were laid out, the meat fitting together like a puzzle. As I munched I was drawn to the look of the flesh on the bone, and I wondered if Tony looked at me that way, like a collection of meat and bones spread out on a bed instead of a tray. If he did he never acted upon it. Tony never barked, bit or nibbled at me but his mouthful of teeth must have been there for a reason.

My train of thought was derailed by a knock on the front door. I was surprised to see Manny standing on the porch. I gulped down my milk and put the glass in the sink then headed for the door. He looked gaunt and thin as if he'd lost weight in just a few days. But his eyes were bright and he seemed to be himself.

"Hey stranger, how are you feeling?"

"Better, at least a little bit."

"Back at school?" I knew school was hard for everyone, not just me. Even Manny, as cool as he was, had hard times with certain things. Everyone had their own monsters.

"Yeah, today was the first day back. I had to make up a ton of work. I'll probably be doing homework until August." He laughed, his eyes darting from me to the house then to me again.

"Do you want to come in?" I said, moving aside. He stepped in hesitantly, taking a few steps from the front door. He looked like he would bolt if a bird sang. He took on a serious look and leaned into me.

"Look, we're still friends. I just got really spooked and it's made me a little crazy. I had night terrors for years and this just kicked it into overdrive," he whispered, as if we were in a crowded room.

"Don't worry about it, Manny."

32

"What's the latest on your live in 'friend'?" he asked, his eyes still darting about.

"I think I have him on video," I boasted.

"Really?"

"Yeah, want to see it?" I teased. Manny looked like I asked him to jump off a building but, despite his obvious fear, he shook his head 'yes.' I left him in the living room while I took the stairs two at a time to get the tape.

****

By the time I returned, I knew it was taking a lot for Manny to stay in the house. The fact that it was daytime helped but Manny still looked scared stiff. I told him that I didn't think adults couldn't see Tony or if they did he would leave. It was all conjecture on my part after all but I had no other ideas. I put the tape in the VCR and pressed "play."

Manny tensed when the image came on the screen. He watched with fascination as the sound in the dark room started banging and then the light. I pointed out the movement of the light, the purr, his claws scratching my dresser and the sound of my stuff hitting the floor. Then there was the close up and the hiss. I played the part with the hiss a few times without saying what I had heard. I was hoping Manny had heard the same thing.

"Did that thing say something?" Manny asked.

"I think he said 'yes;' at least it sounded that way," I said.

"Play it again for me."

I rewound to the right spot.

"YYYYYYEEEEEEEEESSSSSSSSSSSSSSS"

We both looked at each other and I rewound and hit play it again. Once more, *"YYYYYYEEEEEEEEEESSSSSSSSSSSSSSS"*

"Cadence should listen to this," he said.

****

Manny stayed much longer than I thought he would. Maybe he was returning to his old self but I felt like he was trying to face his demons, although I doubted that a sleepover would ever again be in our future.

The next day was Friday and after school, Cadence appeared at the door. She had visited Manny for a short while and he told her she should come to listen to the tape. Mom saw her come and she smiled at both of us, and went inside. I hoped she wouldn't make a big deal out of Cadence being here, but I supposed it was alright if she had the wrong impression. At least that would throw her off our trail.

Mom had put out some Oreos and milk in the kitchen then gone to the laundry room to fold clothes, but she was in earshot of the kitchen, and I could tell she was listening. After small talk and a snack, I took Cadence to the living room. I left my guest alone as I went to retrieve the tape from my dresser drawer.

I set up the tape and pressed "play." She watched intensely, riveted to the screen. The darkness, the banging, the light high in the shot, the purr, my voice, the crash and then the close up with the hiss all played again for us. I played the hiss a few times over hoping Cadence would hear it, too.

"Tony can speak?" she asked.

"I'm still not completely convinced but he may be able to,"

"I think the videotape is good enough to show your folks," she said. I think she wanted them to know regardless of whether the tape was good enough or not.

"I'll show them this weekend, then. I have to return the camera equipment tomorrow, anyway. I'll play it for them after we get home from my grandmother's house."

"If it's early enough, I can come over and show it to them with you," she offered.

"I think it would be better if I did that part by myself. Thank you for the offer, though."

Chapter Eight

On Saturday morning, I was on my way to Grandma's house with Mom and Dad in the back of the Lincoln. She lived on the other side of town only a few miles away. Grandpa had been gone since I was little, so it was always Grandma's house to me. On the seat beside me was the case containing the video equipment. The camera case looked like a hard plastic suitcase complete with a handle. Mom wanted to be sure that I was very appreciative to Grandma and said "thank you" to her as many times as possible.

Grandma and I always got along fine; she made the best pancakes in the world. They were crêpe style and I rolled them up once I covered them in syrup and butter. She made them every time I stayed over. I hadn't slept over her house in a while but I planned on doing so once I figured out what to do about Tony.

We arrived in time for lunch so instead of pancakes, we had pot roast. Fortunately I only had cereal for breakfast so I was hungry. Grandma, as many grandmothers are, was a great cook. Over dinner she asked me what I used the camera for.

I said, "I tape random stuff just to get used to the equipment."

"That's nice," she said. Everything was always nice to Grandma. I hoped she would let me use the camera again.

There was more small talk through dinner and over dessert. Adults could talk about nothing for a long time. Hours later, it was time to leave and I gave Grandma a big hug and kiss like I always did. I always had the suspicious feeling that I was seeing her for the last time when I left her house. I had always been wrong but one day I would be right. Then I would feel her absence; I was hoping that day was still a long way off.

In the car I decided to bring up Tony. I tried an indirect and evasive approach.

"Mom, I was talking to you the other day about a friend I wanted you to meet," I started.

"Yes, I remember," she said. She was splitting her attention between me and Dad. Dad was playing with the radio while he drove.

"He's a special kind of friend. I have him on video tape," I admitted.

"Oh? Well, I'll look at the tape with you when we get home," she said. Dad found a station he liked and we drove the rest of the way without talking. I guess the tape would have to do the talking for me.

＊＊＊＊

Once home I went to my room and retrieved the video tape. Dad was upstairs changing into his sweat pants getting ready to spend the rest of the day in his easy chair reading. He would read everything, newspapers, paperbacks, magazines. I thought if I put a dictionary next to him, he'd pick that up and read it like any other. Mom was puttering about the house putting things away when I put the tape in the VCR and rewound it. I called her.

"Remember the other night when Dad heard a noise from my room and got out of bed?" I asked her as I pushed 'Play'.

"Yes, what is this now? Is this a tape from that night?" She was finally paying full attention and looking at the screen.

"Yes, it's a tape of my friend Tony," I said as the screen darkened and the muffled banging began.

"Tony, who's Tony?" she said while showing interest in the screen. The blurry light appeared high in the frame and the sound of the cloak brushing the closet door followed.

"Why can't I see anything?"

"Hold on, you'll see him." I was looking intently at the screen also. Then there was the lion-like purr as the light grew closer. I heard my voice asking again, "What's your problem?" Then we heard the scraping of the claws and the falling objects followed by the crashing coin jar.

"Hey, what the heck are you doing?" I said on the tape.

I could see that the production was holding her attention and we had reached the part I really wanted her to see. When the light grew on the screen and the hiss began is when I noticed something I hadn't seen before — his eyes.

There were two black circles in the blurry light of Tony's captured image where eyes should be. I had seen the tape about a dozen times by then and I had never noticed the eyes.

"YYYYYYEEEEEEEESSSSSSSSSSSSSSSS"

Then there was the sound of my parents' door opening and Dad trudging down the hall. The light disappeared and was briefly followed by my Dad saying, "What is going on in there?"

I looked at Mom who was looking from the screen to me to the screen again, her eyes stern.

"What is all this? Were you playing tricks on your father?" She sounded accusatory.

"No, no tricks Mom. I was visited by something or *someone*," I pleaded. "I don't even know what it is, that's why I wanted to film it!"

"Are you trying to tell me that you were visited by a ghost?" she asked flatly.

"I'm not sure what it is. It's been here before — dozens of times. I don't even know why." I was losing steam with my argument to make her believe me. She looked at me for a moment; I could see her mind working.

"If you want to make home-made horror movies, that's OK with me; just don't wake us up in the middle of the night. Can't you and your friends do this during the day?"

I couldn't answer her.

She swallowed and said, "It was a good first effort, honey. It was pretty spooky to me." She stood and headed towards the kitchen then turned back and said, "You'll have to tell me how you made the light move and how you made that hissing voice."

What she did next gave me goose bumps. Mom turned, imitating Tony she said, "Yyyyyyeeeeeeeessssssssssssss."

****

I watched the tape a few more times and saw those same eyes in the center of the blurry light. I was convinced that they weren't there before, but I would need confirmation from either Manny or Cadence. I also thought about Tony and tried to think of the last time he appeared blurry and out of focus. Apparently I hadn't noticed. I distinctly remember his early visits being very blurry; I found it hard to tell what shape he was back then. His focused appearance was another change, but more gradual. What was most disturbing was that the image on the video itself seemed to be becoming focused on its own. I wasn't sure how that worked but was sure Tony himself had something to do with it.

I decided to be more observant on his subsequent visits. I put a notebook and pens on the nightstand as well as my flashlight and the camera I got for my birthday the previous year. If all went according to plan, I would soon be 12 and two years from graduation so I also made the decision not to provoke Tony, as his behavior was becoming unpredictable. I would reserve comments and resist involving him in anymore experiments.

Earlier I wouldn't think twice about asking Tony to pick a card from a deck or some other foolishness. I read to Tony — mostly Asimov; I had shown him my homework; I sang to him on more than one occasion; all my efforts received no sign of interest. He only floated and stared, floated and stared.

The only time would he react was when I tried to keep him from leaving. He would scratch something, usually the wall. If I tried to block his way when he began to retreat towards the closet or the foot of the bed, he would scratch at something but never me. If he felt threatened, he never scratched me, just something inanimate. I would always let him go, and whatever scratches he left would be gone by morning. Until his last visit, anyway.

****

That Sunday morning, we went to church as per our usual routine. Unless we were ill, on vacation or at a school event, we went to church. Mom and Dad were both raised Catholic so they raised me the same. I didn't mind. I liked the quiet of the church and the smell of the candles melting. Somehow, the quiet reminded me of the library in a way.

The library, of course, why didn't I think of that sooner? I needed to research the history of our house. I would read any and all articles about our street, our house in particular, to see whether there had been any out of the ordinary events in the area. I was sure this would be the perfect starting point, and hopefully lead to something, some way I could evict Tony.

The library was closed on Sunday so I would have to ask Mom to take me after school on Monday. Hopefully she could leave me there for a couple of hours before dinner. I supposed that I would have to make more than one trip to find something to help me get rid of Tony.

Chapter Nine

*M*om was always happy to bring me to the library, and the next day, she dropped me off and told me that Dad would pick me up on his way home at 5:30. I waved goodbye and entered my sanctuary, breathing in the smells of books and all that knowledge. The library was less than 10 years old, and had that modern look with sharp angles and plenty of glass in the front. But some of the knowledge it held in its pages were eons old.

I loved the place and knew it intimately. I had gone there since I was very little; I would play among the rows while my parents would make their selections. Dad would have piles of books every week, being the avid reader he was, and waiting for him to check out gave me extra time to explore. It wasn't long before I discovered all the wonders kept there including ancient texts saved from the old library. The old library had been a converted church established almost a century ago. It was wooden and one day it caught fire. They saved most of the books and things but the building was a loss.

With the fire in mind, the new library was built with multiple exits, a conference room, water cooler, copy machines and even wheelchair access ramps. There were microfiche machines in the back where they converted most of the area newspapers for storage. Works from the town's art museum were displayed in the upstairs corridors between conference rooms, offices and storage spaces. The library also had many volumes of printed books dating back hundreds of years, some donated by anonymous philanthropists.

The librarian on duty was Mrs. White, an older lady who worked part time. We had gotten to know each other over the years. She loved books and told me she had started working there once all of her children were grown and gone. Even though she knew me, the microfiche machines were in a secure area so she had to authorize usage. I handed her my library card, which she would keep until I was done.

I told her I was working on a report for school about the town and she directed me to the local archives. She smiled and left, allowing me to search on my own, which suited me perfectly.

Once she was out of sight, I started my search. The microfiche contained several newspapers including *The Sentinel*, the town paper which was very small, but still it would take me weeks to go over the decades the town had steadily recorded its goings on. Just because it was a small paper with a small circulation didn't mean the town news wasn't worth recording, and record they did. The remaining papers were of much larger circulation. For the moment, I would focus on the closest paper to the home.

I began with a random date of March 2, 1955; on page 5 there was an article about the sale of Atkins' Pig Farm off of West Street. West Street was a main road near my house and I didn't know that there was ever a pig farm there. The article said that Mr. Atkins had died several months earlier and Mrs. Atkins was selling the place to go live with her daughter and her son in-law. It was all very interesting but not what I thought I was looking for. I tried to not get lost reading all the old stories of house fires or people gone missing, because I knew I'd become intrigued and spend hours trying to hunt down the follow up article where the missing person had been located, forgetting to tell relatives that they'd gone on vacation or something silly like that.

Several tapes later I was in June of 1962. There was another series of articles about a new housing development off West Street at the site of Atkins Farm. A little more reading confirmed that it was Atkins' Pig Farm. One article had a picture of bulldozers clearing some land.

A couple of tapes later recounted May 1964, when the housing development was close to completion and several homes were not only sold but occupied. There was also a photograph of a raised ranch style home; it had to be brand new as there were no trees or shrubs planted yet. The landscape aside the house and the newly paved driveway, was barren, and I recognized the house. It was my house, *our house*.

The article never mentioned the owner's name so I would have to ask Mrs. White if that kind of information was available at the library but I guessed I would probably have to go to town hall. I was trying to speed read while mainly looking at headlines. I was burning a lot of time and knew Dad would be there soon.

I caught the article by accident; it was on the lower second page of the paper dated November 9, 1972. I don't know why I stopped to read the article but my eyes were instantly drawn to the headline. Nothing was exceptional about the article at all, except the terrible story it told. The article was short and had no accompanying photos.

Local Boy Loses Battle with Brain Cancer
Jack Sterns

Anthony Delmarre, age 8, died yesterday at the Saint Peter Memorial Hospital. He was born February 14, 1964 and attended Chemung Elementary School. Anthony was a second year Cub Scout of Troop 18 and a member of the local Little League team, The Bears.
Anthony is survived by his parents Joseph and Louise Delmarre, his sister Maria, his grandfather Anthony Delmarre, as well as several aunts, uncles and cousins.
Funeral arrangements are being handled by the Farley Funeral Home. Services will be held Saturday at 2-4pm and again at 7-9pm. The Funeral will be held on Sunday at 9am at the Lady of the Rosary Church. The procession will follow ending at Mount Olive Cemetery.

I read it several times, something was not right and it took my mind time begin to reason it out. It struck me like those "Eureka" moments in a cartoon when a light bulb appears over the characters head. The boys name was Anthony Delmarre; Anthony. Tony was short for Anthony. It was a stretch, more of a long shot, but I had a feeling about it just the same.

I was not one to experience intuition all too often. I needed facts and figures, something more tangible. It was a lead, however small, and I decided to investigate it. The remaining tapes had no further information on poor little Anthony Delmarre. I would have to do some foot work; I would canvass the neighborhood and ask if anyone knew the Delmarres.

I was done with the microfiche for the day; I turned it off and returned the tapes to their appropriate places. My Dad's would arrive any minute so I returned my library card to Mrs. White and told her that I cleaned up and secured everything. As soon as she smiled at me, I asked her, "Did you ever know a boy named Anthony Delmarre?"

She thought for a moment and answered, "No, I can't say that I have."

"Can I get a history of home ownership here at the library or is that kept at town hall?" I inquired.

"Oh, that's at town hall." She looked to me awaiting another question but I had gathered my things and was heading for the door.

****

Dad and I arrived home in time for a spaghetti dinner; it was Italian, which seemed appropriate. During our dinner conversation, I arranged with Mom and Dad to go to the library again the next day. After dinner I volunteered to bring the garbage to the outside container.

After I deposited the stinky bag into the can I went to the garage. Dad kept a large flashlight in there that was more powerful than the average kind. It required a big battery that was square, about 5 inches tall and weighed a couple of pounds. It cast almost as much light as the electric light that came with the video camera.

Tony had been scared off by a bright light before so if there was trouble the flashlight might provide some security. If things continued to get out of hand, I was going to start sleeping with the lights on, which might halt his visits altogether.

43

First, I needed more answers to my questions. I needed to know if Tony could really speak or if I was imagining things during his last visit. I needed to know how and why Tony was becoming clearer both on tape and in person. He hadn't been "out of focus" for me for quite some time and on the tape his face was becoming clearer as well.

I also wanted to know more about the Delmarre family and their son, Anthony. What happened to the family after Anthony died? Were they still in town? He had a sister, Marie, and I would certainly love to talk to her about him. I wondered where she was. Finally, I wanted to know more about Atkins Pig Farm, after all, I was living on it. How long had it been there and what was there before it?

Most importantly, I needed to find a way to deal with Tony. Why had his formerly unremarkable visits turned aggressive? Would this escalate to violence? I had never before feared Tony but I was beginning to feel uneasy. As a matter of fact, for the longest time, I considered him my friend. Fear was new to me and I didn't like the feeling one bit.

As I went through the motions of preparing for bed, I was lost in thought. Before I came up to my room, I said goodnight to Dad, his nose in a book as usual. Mom came to my room and gave me a kiss on the cheek.

She noticed the flashlight. "Do you have some more nocturnal activities planned?" she asked, pointing at the flashlight.

"No, nothing planned. I just wanted to keep it next to my bed," I answered sleepily.

"You're a little old to be afraid of the dark, aren't you?" She smiled.

"I'm not afraid of the dark, Mom. Besides, you leave the bathroom light on every night."

"Alright then, goodnight," she said as she hugged me. "But whatever you're doing in your closet, it's leaving a lot of scratch marks on the door. You should knock that off; Dad won't be happy if he has to refinish it or replace it."

She left the room and as soon as I heard the bathroom door close behind her, I went to the closet with the big flashlight in hand and opened it. On the back of the door were many little scratches, like a dog had worked it over trying to get out. But, a dog would have to have been tall, as the scratches went from the bottom of the door to the top.

I closed the door and went to the bed where I got down on the floor and brought the light underneath. My things were pushed up to one end of the bed where my pillow was and there were scratches there as well. More physical evidence from Tony. I turned off the light and put it back on the nightstand. I turned off the light in the room and went to bed; sleep did not come for some time.

Tony did not visit, which was not that unusual. There was no rhyme or reason to his visits; Tony did not follow a schedule. At some point, I finally fell asleep, but it seemed like I was up until dawn.

Chapter Ten

*M*om let me out on the front sidewalk in front of the library again the next day. As I watched her Volvo drive away, I began walking towards the center of town.

Two main roads passed directly through the town center forming an X: Routes 37 and Route 148. Route 148 ran northeast to southwest, like a diagonal on a compass and Route 37 ran northwest to the southeast, another diagonal This unorganized road system was the result of horse and buggy travel, a lack of vision that, as the years carried on, created an epic traffic standoff in the center during the morning commute and again in the late afternoon. Locals would avoid the center at those times at all costs.

The town was established long before the country's official birth in 1776, and had been a settlement of farmers and craftsmen. Later, through the 1800s, shoe factories appeared and the town grew rapidly, and was bolstered by contracts supplying Union soldiers with footwear.

The town's Historical Society Museum was a converted bank with the date 1920 carved into its cornerstone. Dad was a Society member and I had visited the museum several times before. According to Mr. Green, who ran the Society, the stonework and foundation were laid for the vault and then the bank was constructed around it. It was a brilliant idea as the vault weighed many tons and was too massive even for modern day machinery. It remained in the building and was viewable as soon as one entered. The door to the vault was always left open and was available for inspection by any patron during business hours. The vault was right out of the movies; it was made of shiny metal and the large, heavy door had a wheel like knob to open it. I was fascinated by it.

The teller's counter was long ago removed as were the wrought iron bars designed to protect them. The remainder of the Historical Society Museum was laid out in converted offices and conference areas. Objects included many maps hung on the walls and Revolutionary era documents on parchment kept under glass. There was an authentic Militia Man's coat, boots from another soldier of the era and a pair of spectacles supposedly belonging to George Washington. Washington had allegedly slept the night at the Grist Mill Tavern which still remained on the edge of town but I had my doubts. Washington supposedly slept everywhere.

I went to the maps and through them, began to trace the history of the West Street area where my neighborhood now stands. The maps indeed showed Atkins Pig Farm but on earlier maps there was nothing noted in the area but West Street itself. I sought out Mr. Green who was in the back preparing a presentation for members of the Society on the history of Reed's Pond. Reed's Pond was the town's public swimming area. I had taken swimming lessons there since I was five years old.

"Mr. Green, would you happen to know the history of Atkins' Pig Farm? I was looking at the maps and it seems to go back two hundred years but before that nothing is listed."

Mr. Green was pleasant but he was all business, and continued writing while I stood there.

Maybe lifting his head was too much effort for him. He looked to be a hundred years old to me but in reality he was probably in his 70s. He always dressed in a collared shirt, suspenders and a bow tie. He had a thin, white mustache like the ones movie stars wore in the 1930s. He also knew everything about the town and claimed to be related to a member of the Sons of Liberty.

Mr. Green finished what he was writing and looked up at me, "Young man, I can tell you everything about Atkins Farm; I personally knew Mr. Atkins." He put down his pen and stood, leading me back to the maps on the wall. "Mr. Atkins was the fourth generation to farm that land and sell hay and livestock, mostly pigs. The livestock went mainly to A&P Grocery Stores and the hay went to local municipalities."

"What would the municipalities want with the hay?" I said, trying not to stare at his little mustache.

"They not only fed their horses, which was their chief mode of transportation until this century; they also used the hay to barricade road projects. Some of the hay was used in treating the dirt roads themselves." He said never taking his eyes from the map. The map was dated 1775 to 1875 which clearly showed the farm as well as the town; the town was a fraction of its current size.

"What was the land used for before Atkins' Farm?" I was ready for my lesson.

"The Atkins Family emigrated from England in the 1760s and settled here. They were servants of an English Lord that helped them finance their purchase of the land from the British government before arriving. It was rumored that the Lord had married one of the family's daughters, which was scandalous for those times; she was considered by society to be beneath his social strata. To keep them quiet, the Lord assisted them in their relocation; the whole family was sent to America aside from the newly wed daughter, of course."

"Of course," I interrupted. Mr. Green didn't seem to notice, he was on a roll.

"Though the land was claimed by the British government, it belonged to the Namtuxet tribe as did the whole town as well as the surrounding towns, possibly more. The Namtuxet lived here for hundreds, if not thousands, of years. They were a peaceful tribe of farmers, hunters and gatherers who lived in small, wooden structures for several seasons before moving on."

"Was there any evidence of the Namtuxet ever found on Atkins' Farm?" I prodded.

"Of course; though the temporary shelters constructed of tree limbs, bark and mud would return to nature not long after they were abandoned, there are also many stone structures left by the natives throughout the area. Their markings would be painted or carved into the stone."

"What would the stone structures be used for?"

"For one, the Namtuxet would build stone fire pits for warmth and cooking. Another construction would be for storage. Caves or man-made dugouts would shelter a great deal of things from the elements. The Namtuxet would also mark their gravesites with stone structures."

"Gravesites?" My interest piqued.

"Yes, they buried their dead and typically marked the area with a wooden or stone ornament. They would leave items for the dead to take with them on their journey into the afterlife and write messages of farewell on the wooden or stone markers."

"Were any of these gravesites found on Atkins Farm?" I asked.

"It's hard to say. There were stones with markings that local scholars believed to be evidence of a burial site, and I know the Atkins family never disturbed the few they suspected were burial sites, and farmed around them. When the farm was sold in the 1950s to a local developer, some local scholars and historians tried to stop the construction on the site claiming that it was a Native American burial ground with historical significance. Eventually, the developer won. It was a different time then." Mr. Green finally turned to look at me.

"Did they ever find anything during construction?" I asked.

"If you mean pottery or bones or that sort of thing the answer is 'No'. But, the developer did donate the stones to one of the area colleges for further study."

"What did you think of the whole thing, the development and all?" I asked him.

"I'm not one who likes change very much," he said smiling. Then he added, "why the interest in Atkins Farm?"

"I believe that the development in question is my neighborhood, Mr. Green."

Mr. Green smiled broadly at that then he began to shuffle back to his desk. "I hope I've answered your questions satisfactorily," he said.

"Yes, but I have one more," I said, and he stopped and turned.

"Did you ever know a boy named Anthony Delmarre?" I asked.

He stopped to think then answered, "Ah yes, the poor boy who passed at such a young age. He was very sick, indeed. Why do you ask?"

"Oh, I just ran across the article recently. Thanks for your time, Mr. Green. I'll be back sometime soon," I said as I started for the door.

I could hear Mr. Green say to me, "The Delmarre's were from your neighborhood before they moved away. I don't know where they are now but I hope they are well. Anyway, tell your father I asked for him."

I stopped at the door and turned. "I will." I walked back to the library and scoured more microfiche until my father came to pick me up.

Chapter Eleven

𝔇inner, homework, bedtime; I kept to my regular weekday routine. After brushing my teeth and saying my goodnights I returned to my room to prepare. Tony hadn't been by and he was due; I was certain he would come that night. I checked the big flashlight on the night stand as well as the closet. I used the flashlight and looked under the bed; nothing.

I turned off the light and left the door ajar as I always had. The only light came from the bathroom down the hall. I rarely had to go to the bathroom in the middle of the night and was unaware of anyone else in the family doing so either but Mom insisted it stay on "just in case."

I liked having the door ajar so that I could hear Dad getting ready for work. Dad left earlier than we did and he wasn't the quietest about it, but I liked hearing him. It was the only time of day he used the television with such regularity. He watched about 15 minutes of the morning news to get an update on his commute and the weather for the day.

As I lay in my room with the covers pulled up neatly about me, I thought of Cadence. I hadn't spoken to her in a few days and was unhappy about it. I thought of all of the things I had discovered and needed to share with her. I wondered if she had been keeping Manny company. Manny really needed to be with people; he was still a bit flustered and suffered from his night terrors.

For that, Cadence was the perfect companion; she was very empathetic and was also a good listener. Part of me wanted Cadence to stop seeing Manny and to come to my house regularly instead. I had things to tell her, I enjoyed her company too and I, also, could be a good listener. I needed her.

But I knew Cadence would come by when she was ready, and she would. She wanted to see the "Tony issue" resolved. She was concerned for Manny but she was scared for me. That thought made me smile a little. Cadence was scared for me because she cared. Even Manny cared, but he had his own problems that overshadowed mine.

Then another thought came that alarmed me. What would happen when Tony was finally gone? Would Cadence still talk to me, would Manny? Why were things so complicated? And, would Tony ever really be gone? I fell asleep with questions rolling through my head. What if Tony never left?

****

Bang, clang, scraaaaaaaape. The bed jerked upward and my eyes opened. The performance had begun and it already was shaping up to be a classic. Tony had never moved the bed; maybe he couldn't until then. Maybe he was working out. I was on my back still neatly under the covers. I could see the outline of my legs slightly spread into a V and my toes pointing towards the ceiling. Then there was crunching noises and ripping sounds like someone was shredding a shirt.

The covers began to slowly rise between my legs several inches south of my groin. The covers continued to rise upwards until they were taut, and then a claw broke through. The covers deflated around the protruding claw as it rose almost a foot above them. Then it receded at the same pace it had risen. I realized I had been frozen, still unable to take my eyes away from the foot of the bed. And just like that, I unfroze and pulled my legs up to my chest, wrapping my arms around them.

Both sets of claws appeared on the foot of the bed again. Tony was pulling himself up. His glowing face rose above the bed like a balloon. He looked more animated than before, his mouth was moving, opening and closing like a fish trying to breath out of water. Then he said something.

"MMMMMMIIIIIIIINNNNNNNNNNNNEEEEEEEEEEE."

The voice was like the roar of a lion, deep and powerful. I was surprised that my parents didn't hear it. Tony was suddenly very tall, and towered above me. He stretched out his arms to display magnificent claws on each hand, and he wiggled them slightly. Even in the dim light, Tony cast a clear shadow on the bedroom wall, a shadow that would have made any horror movie fan delighted.

"MMMMMMIIIIIIIINNNNNNNNNNNEEEEEEEEEE."

Tony was indeed in rare form and he was finally able to scare me after all the years of trying. It wasn't his appearance that was scary; it was his new physical manifestation. He had just ripped through my bed and he could probably rip through just about anything, including me. He stood there basking in my horror, I needed to do something.

"Tony, what are you doing?" I yell-whispered at him. I still didn't want my parents to wake up unless it was absolutely necessary. If they heard a commotion and Tony was gone again before they arrived I would be in trouble. Tony began to move towards me.

"Anthony Delmarre!" I said aloud, though not a shout. Tony stopped. He heard me so I kept at it. "Do you know Anthony Delmarre?" Still he had no response but his mouth had closed.

Then Tony moved swiftly and he was upon me in an instant. He brought his face up to mine, inches away from touching. The dark holes of his eyes showed no light and seemed to go on forever. He spoke again in a deep, guttural voice but softly and slowly.

"Mine" was all he said. It was enough.

I dove to my right for the night stand and reached for the flashlight. I turned on the light and brought my hand around, pointing the light at him. The light filled the room, my eyes were unadjusted but I saw what I needed to. Tony disappeared again.

I turned on the light switch and the overhead light filled the room. I turned on my desk lamp as well. I left the flashlight on and propped it up on the night stand; it was aimed at the ceiling. When I was very little, my Dad would do this and make shadow puppets on the ceiling. The white of the ceiling would reflect a lot of the light around the room, if the electricity failed for some reason that light would be more than adequate.

I returned to my bed and tried to restore the covers, there was a three-inch hole in them. There was a hole in my sheets and a bigger hole in the mattress. If I checked I would find a hole in the box spring as well. I put my finger in the hole in the mattress, the hole was neatly cut.

I got back into bed leaving all of the lights on. I covered myself and my last thoughts before sleep was of Cadence. I had even more things to tell her.

Chapter 12

"Good morning, Step," Dad said standing in my doorway. He looked around and added, "Slept with the lights on, I see."

"Hi Dad, I guess I fell asleep with them on." I sat upright. The bed was tussled so the holes were hidden, albeit temporarily.

"Is that my flashlight on your nightstand?" he asked.

"Yes." I wasn't in the mood to explain, at least not yet.

"I see that it's been left on, I assume, all night," he said. I was unsure if he required a response so I didn't offer one. "Are you alright, son?"

"Yes, Dad; I just fell asleep while reading," I offered. This was plausible as I had dozens upon dozens of books in my room and a few kept bed side regularly.

"I'll see you later," he said and turned to leave. I heard his footsteps down the staircase and then the television turned on. I could hear the high pitch whine from the set but not anything being said. The volume must have been set very low.

I got out of bed and got dressed into my day clothes; I usually showered the night before to save time in the morning. As I made the bed I could see the holes in the covers and the mattress. I finished the bed and retrieved a hand-knitted blanket from the top shelf in my closet. The blanket was given to me by my grandmother during her knitting phase and she did a fine job of it. Mom used to fold it and leave it at the foot of my bed as a homey decoration of sorts. When I reached 10 years old, I grew tired of it and retired it to the closet.

But it was the perfect thing to use to cover the hole, so I decided to restore the tradition and spread the blanket on top of the bed spread. Hopefully it would be enough to buy some time before my mother discovered the hole and I would have to explain. I looked under the bed. It was scratched much more than before, as if someone under there had a fit with a carving knife.

I finished cleaning my room and headed downstairs. I poured myself a bowl of Cheerios and joined Dad for breakfast. We ate in silence while the weatherman on the television told us how beautiful the day was going to be.

Dad put his bowl in the sink and grabbed his briefcase. While he slipped on his sport coat, he kissed the top of my head and went to the door. This was a bit abnormal as Dad was never the touchy feely type. He rarely hugged and kissed anyone but Mom; Mom was the one that hugged and kissed with regularity. Mom yelled down the stairs from the bathroom her goodbyes. Dad answered and left; and then Mom and I left for school 20 minutes later.

Mom seemed extra perky on the ride; she sang along with the radio and gave me a big kiss when she dropped me off. Like Dad, I was not fond of public showing of affection; it made me uncomfortable and she knew it but she did it anyway, whether I liked it or not. I made my escape and headed for the entrance and hoped she would be under control when she came to pick me up.

****

Mom was more controlled when she picked me up from school even though she was still perkier than usual. I kept my quiet reserve all the way home but felt my heart skip a beat when I saw Cadence waiting for me on the front porch. Her bike lay on its side, she was dressed in denim shorts and an oversized white t-shirt that said "Relax" on the front; her hair fell onto her shoulders.

Mom gave me a smile and a nod as she went into the house. I watched her go to make sure she was at least out of earshot. I then focused my attention on Cadence and began with, "How's Manny?"

"He's doing a little better. He went back to the doctor and the doctor prescribed something for him," she said.

"Sleeping pills or something," I guessed.

"Something for anxiety. He said they make him slow like he's sleepwalking. After the first one, he said he didn't like feeling that way so he cuts the pills in half." She advised; I changed the subject.

"I have a lot to tell you about Tony," I said.

"I take it he isn't gone yet?" She seemed disappointed.

"No, it's taking longer than I expected to figure this all out. I started at the library and read about our neighborhood. It turns out that Atkins Pig Farm was here before they built this development. I even saw a picture of my house taken when people first began to occupy the new houses. I wanted to know more about Atkins Farm so I went to the Historical Society the next day to ask Mr. Green. He told me that the Atkins family came here from England in the 1760s and settled the farm."

"What does this have to do with Tony?" she interrupted.

"I'm telling you, just listen. Before the Atkins family and even before the town, there was a tribe of Native Americans here called the Namtuxet. They were farmers and hunter/gatherers who occupied this land for thousands of years."

"We learned about them in school," she interrupted again. I tried not to look annoyed but I wished she was more patient.

"Yes, but did you know that they also *buried their dead* on this land? There were stone markers where the possible gravesites were located. Several were found on Atkins Farm and the Atkins family never disturbed them. The developer did; he sent the stone markers to the college for study."

"Did they dig up bodies?" she asked.

"Good question. No, from what I understand, they did not remove the bodies."

"Are we getting to Tony?" She was getting impatient.

"Yes, we are getting to Tony. Like I said, I'm not sure how the Namtuxet tie into this but I have a hunch that they do. I'm investigating all of my leads. Now hold on, there's more; much more," I said, as she turned away.

"Do you think Tony is one of the Namtuxet angry over the loss of their lands?" she asked.

"It's a possibility but it doesn't connect, at least not yet. But here is something more interesting. I also found an article on a kid named Anthony Delmarre. From what I learned, he lived in this neighborhood. He died from some kind of brain tumor back in 1972. I still don't know the connection but I have a feeling that our Tony either knew the Delmarre kid or he may even *be* Tony. Then again, Tony could also be a Namtuxet or something else altogether."

"That's a lot of research in such a short time. You're pretty good at this," she said trying to sound encouraging. I appreciated her effort.

"Wait until you hear the rest," I said.

"There's more?"

"Much more. It's Tony; he's *changing*."

"Changing? How?"

"He's becoming *clearer*," I said. "Follow me and I'll show you," I walked into the house and Cadence followed.

****

Mom was already making us a snack. Cadence went to the kitchen to say hello and talk to Mom, while I ran up to my bedroom to retrieve the videotape. I went into the living room, popped the tape into the VCR, and called Cadence. She came in carrying a plate of Oreos and two glasses of milk. Mom stayed in the kitchen, busy preparing supper.

"You haven't seen the tape yet," I started.

"No, but Manny did. It spooked him a little but he was still able to tell me about it."

"What did he tell you?"

"He said that it was a visit several nights ago and it was blurry. He said that it happened very quickly and it was hard to determine what was really happening."

"He's right, for the most part. Watch." I pushed the tape in and pressed 'Play'. I had the volume low and we were close to the television. The scraping noises began and then Tony's face appeared small and high on the screen. It was no longer blurry; eyes and mouth were clearly visible. As he floated towards the camera his robe was discernible from the dark background. *"What's your problem"* played on the tape and Tony's clawed hand reached out, knocking the items from the dresser. The coin jar crashed. *"Hey, what the heck are you doing?"* I heard myself say.

Tony's face grew as it neared the camera followed by his hiss.

"YYYYYYEEEEEEEESSSSSSSSSSSSSSS"

Then followed the sound of Dad coming down the hallway, and Tony disappeared. I stopped the tape there and looked to Cadence, to see what she thought.

"You have Tony on tape and he spoke." she said in a matter-of-fact tone.

"Yes, but he's not blurry anymore, is he?" I said.

"No, he's not blurry. But Manny said that his face was very blurry, like the film was unfocused."

"He's pretty focused now." I said pulling the tape from the player. "I think he's becoming 'focused' in reality as well."

"What does that mean?"

"He used to be blurry to me during his early visits. Over time his appearance cleared up like it developed. He never said anything or did anything before but now he's able to say things and touch things, break things. You just saw him say 'yes' right to my face. He's stretching or growing, becoming more *real*."

"Has he said something else?" She looked amazed.

"Last night was his most violent visit yet. He ripped right through my bed, box spring and all. Then he came right up to me and said, 'Mine'. The flashlight scared him off; I had to sleep with the lights on so he wouldn't come back," I said, turning off the television.

"I told you he was dangerous," Cadence said looking a little angry with me. Her eyes darted back and forth so she could scold me without my mother hearing. "He may do something to hurt you. We need to figure out a way to make him leave."

"What do you think I've been doing? I need a little more time; I think I can figure it out. Until I'm ready to see him again I plan on sleeping with the lights on. Now follow me come see my room for a minute so I can show you the hole in the bed."

We sneaked upstairs to my room. I put the tape safely away then went to the bed and pulled back the knitted blanket. There was a neat, three-inch slit in the bedspread. I stuck my finger in it to demonstrate how deep it was. I pulled the spread back to show the hole in the mattress. Cadence shook her head in amazement while I returned the spread and the blanket, smoothing it out into place.

"I think you need some help with this," Cadence whispered. She looked scared.

"What do you have in mind?" I asked.

"This is your investigation; *you* tell me what *you* need," she offered. I thought about it and the next thing on my checklist was Anthony Delmarre. We sneaked back down the stairs to the living room. Mom was still in the kitchen busy at the blender.

"We need to find someone who knew Anthony Delmarre or the family, and find out which house was theirs. There may be something at the house that Tony wants or needs, a talisman of some sort. Something like the Namtuxet markers," I told her.

Cadence thought for a moment. "What would Tony's talisman look like?" she asked.

"I don't know but I think we should know once we find it," I said.

"That doesn't help narrow it down," she quipped.

"I know, but that's all I've got for the moment. Let's think. Who's been in the neighborhood long enough to know the Delmarre family?" I asked.

"There are a couple of people on my street; the Rose family, Mr. Topaz," she began.

"Mr. Topaz has been here since the beginning, hasn't he?" I asked even though I knew the answer.

"I think so," she said.

"Alright then, let's start with Mr. Topaz," I said.

I went to the kitchen and told my mother that we were going outside for a while. She told me to be back in time for dinner and I agreed. We left the house and Cadence picked up her bike. She walked along side of me pushing the bike while I stole glances at her; I was unable to help myself.

We walked like that all the way to see Mr. Topaz.

Chapter 13

*W*e approached Mr. Topaz's house, which was a Cape covered in white vinyl siding and had black vinyl shutters. The lawn and shrubs were kept tidy and a tan Ford Crown Victoria was parked in the driveway. At the back of the driveway, there was a basketball net and, in the back yard, was a swing set. Cadence stopped me on the sidewalk before we went up to the door.

"Have you ever met Mr. Topaz?" she asked.

"No. I haven't," I said looking at her eyes. "I guess I'm not that social."

"That's OK; I'll do most of the talking if you want." She smiled.

"Don't worry; I'll jump in when I deem it necessary." I smiled back. "What's Mr. Topaz like?"

"He's very nice; he's older like my grandfather. He's a widow. I think his wife died a few years ago and his two sons are grown up and are off with their own families."

"Why is he still here, in this town?" I said looking around.

Cadence looked to the house and said "Maybe he wants to be. You don't have to have a family to live somewhere."

She rang the doorbell and stepped back on the porch. I stood back on the walkway holding Cadence's bike and watching her. The door opened and a grandfatherly gentleman greeted her.

"Hello, Cadence." He smiled at her; it seemed like the whole world smiled at her.

"Hi, Mr. Topaz. I was hoping I could ask you a few questions about the neighborhood if you have a moment?" she said sheepishly.

"Of course. What kind of questions?" he said, still smiling at her.

I stepped forward and took control of the conversation to move it along. "Would you know a kid named Anthony Delmarre?"

Mr. Topaz stopped smiling as soon as she said the name. He answered, "Why yes, I remember the Delmarre family."

Cadence cleared her throat and jumped in, "Would you know what happened to Anthony's folks, Mr. Topaz?" He looked over her shoulder, towards me, with a very serious look on his face. He wasn't smiling. Then his attention returned to her and the smile returned as well.

"Why are you asking me about the Delmarre family, Cadence? Is someone looking for them?"

"No one is looking for them; we just wanted to find someone that could tell us what happened to them," I said, taking the smile from Mr. Topaz again.

"What is this about, Cadence?" he said, looking at her this time without smiling.

"It's not her fault, Mr. Topaz; it's me. I ran across an article about Anthony while doing some research at the library and I wanted to know more. We figured we would ask any of the neighbors that had been around long enough to remember them. That's all."

He sighed as if thinking it over; then he said, "Well, the Delmarre's bought their house around the same time I bought mine. Joe Delmarre worked as a surveyor for the town and I was a police officer. Joe and Louise, Mrs. Delmarre, were still newlyweds when they bought the house in 1964. My wife and I knew them even before they moved here. We even went to their wedding. When they bought the house, Louise was expecting and Joe was in the right place at the right time."

Mr. Topaz was looking back and forth between Cadence and me while he spoke. "We were good friends," he added.

"What about the baby, Mr. Topaz?" Cadence gently urged him on.

"The baby was born some months later. It was a boy; Anthony. He was a good kid. Joe and Louise were proud. They were a happy family. Maria, their daughter, was born a couple of years later. Then Tony, they called him Tony, became sick when he was about 7 or 8. It was awful for them, for everyone. Within a year he was gone," Mr. Topaz looked away for a while, then seemed to remember we were there. "Why do you want to know this stuff, anyway?" He sounded angry.

"Like I said, Mr. Topaz, I read the article and Mr. Green from the Historical Society mentioned that he lived in this neighborhood when I asked him," I explained again.

"Mr. Green, huh? Good old Alvin knows everything about everything," Mr. Topaz said with no smile. "Well, Mr. Green didn't know the Delmarres like I knew the Delmarres. Sometimes he's just full of crap. Sorry Cadence." He looked down at her; she gently shook her head but said nothing.

"I'm a member of the Historical Society, too," he said. Then pointing at me, he said "I know you and your father from there. Your father is a good man, very smart."

After a moment he continued, "The last time I saw little Tony was Halloween night, weeks before he…well, you know. He was sick and had doctors and nurses coming to the house almost every day. He could barely walk; they had stopped his chemotherapy by then." Mr. Topaz had to stop, he was getting misty eyed. He took a deep breath and went on.

"Tony was a determined little kid and he wanted to go out for Trick or Treat no matter what. It was his favorite holiday and he wanted his candy. Louise put him in his costume and Joe took him to a few houses in the neighborhood including ours. Joe had to carry little Tony the whole way. My wife gave him practically all the candy in the house. A day or two later he was sent to the hospital and never came home. Not long after that Joe, Louise and Maria moved away, heartbroken. I never saw them again."

"What was his costume?" I asked Mr. Topaz.

"His what?" Mr. Topaz seemed irritated. He'd seemed miles away.

"What was his costume?" I said again. Mr. Topaz looked at me like I was a bug on his shoe.

"He was the Phantom of the Opera like that Lon Chaney movie in the '20s or '30s. He liked that kind of thing — scary movies. Louise made the cape for him and Joe got the little white mask mail order from New York somewhere. It feels like it was just yesterday," Mr. Topaz trailed off again.

Phantom of the Opera, white mask and black cape; I could see the realization in Cadence's eyes as she connected the dots. Mr. Topaz was at the end of his patience with us, "OK kids, that's enough. I'm going back inside. Cadence, it is always a pleasure. As for you young man, you need to work on your manners."

"Which house was his, Mr. Topaz?" I said as he was turning to close the door.

He looked back at me and said, "They used to own your house," then he closed the door.

Chapter 14

$\mathcal{J}$ pushed Cadence's bicycle for her as I walked her home. We looked nervously at each other before saying anything. I got the ball rolling. "Tony is little Anthony Delmarre, I know he is."

"I think you're right but what's made him come back? I mean, he's dead isn't he?" She looked to me for the answer.

"I'm not sure why he came back; maybe he never left at all," I said, but I was guessing.

"If he never left that would be so sad. He never got to Heaven and joined his family up there waiting for him. That might explain why he's acting out the way he is."

"Maybe. Then again maybe there is no Heaven and we all just roam the Earth after our bodies die," I said. As I looked up, I caught a glimpse of her red lips. I loved to watch them move when she spoke.

"Don't say that! There has to be a Heaven; there just has to be!" Cadence's face looked like she ate something sour; tears were forming in those big, blue eyes.

"Sorry Cadence, I'm not trying to upset you," I said.

"That's OK. It's not you upsetting me. I'm just a little upset about the whole thing." She forced a smile. "What are we going to do next?"

I wanted to spend more time with Cadence, but we'd reached her house too soon. As we neared her front yard, I considered our next steps.

"For starters, I'm going to have another talk with my parents this evening. I want to know who owned our house after the Delmarres, because we didn't move in until four years after Anthony Delmarre died," I said as we stood on her front walk.

She took the bicycle from me and asked, "What about the talisman? Are there any in your yard?"

"I never found any but I didn't really look. That's a good idea though. Could you come by tomorrow after school and help me look?" I asked her, feeling the heat in my collar rise and hoping she didn't notice.

"Sure, I can do that. Maybe we should get Manny to help too."

"I don't want him to freak out by being at my house. We can visit him if we find something and bring him up to date on the 'Tony situation'," I countered. The last thing I wanted when I was with Cadence was Manny's presence.

"What about tonight? What if Tony comes?" Cadence looked worried.

"I'm going to sleep with the lights on again," I said.

She thought about that for a moment and seemed more at ease. "Good. I'll see you tomorrow," she said and took her bike to the back of the house.

"Tomorrow...," I said to no one but myself.

****

I returned home and got ready for dinner. The house smelled of garlic and other spices. Mom was whipping up a large dinner. She smiled wide when she saw me and asked me about Cadence. I gave her my one raised eyebrow look as if she was peculiar but said nothing. I went to my room to finish some homework before dinner was ready. I heard Dad return home and soon the three of us were at the kitchen table. Mom had concocted a meatloaf that actually looked inviting and, after grace, everyone was eating like they were starving. I waited for the opportunity to ask them about the former owners of the house. Unfortunately, I waited too long.

"Your mother and I have been back to Dr. Erkahn," Dad started. I stopped eating, waiting for some explanation of where this would lead. "We thought that it might be good for you to start seeing him again."

"We're just a little concerned about you, honey; we want you to have someone to talk to and work things out," Mom added.

"What are your concerns?" I asked in a business-like tone.

"Well, the positives are that you've actually made friends over the past months, which is great! They're good kids and we like them," Mom started.

"And your school work has never suffered so we're proud of that too," Dad volunteered.

"You've given me the things you liked. What are the things that you don't?" I was genuinely curious. I thought that I had come out of my shell in a spectacular fashion. It required serious effort on my part and I had hoped they had noticed and appreciated me for it.

"Well...there are the nightmares for starters. You're up more in the middle of the night now than you've ever been," Dad said, taking a bite of meatloaf. "Including when you were little."

"Yes, sweetie, and we want to know what you're doing up there at night. You've damaged your furniture and your closet door. Dr. Erkahn is concerned...we are worried that you might start hurting yourself," Mom said.

They waited for me to reply, and I kept them waiting a moment to take a bite of potatoes.

"When do I begin therapy?" I asked.

"Next Tuesday after school," Dad said. "I thought we'd try it again for a while and see how things go."

"What do you think of this, sweetie?" Mom asked hopefully.

"Yeah, sure," was all I could say. I went back to eating and Dad did too. Mom watched me for a little while longer, then starting eating again too.

****

After dinner Dad went to his easy chair and read the paper while Mom cleaned up the dishes and the table. I went to see him to find out about our house and the previous owners.

"Dad, who were the people living here when you and Mom bought the house?" I said to the newspaper in which his nose was buried.

Without skipping a beat he answered, "The Millers." Well, at least he knew that much. I figured I would pry more from him.

"What happened to the Millers, Dad?"

"They moved away about a year before we bought the house." His voice still came from behind the newspaper.

"So no one was living here until we moved in?"

"Nope, no one. Mrs. Miller had a breakdown or something and the family had to leave."

"What kind of breakdown?"

"I'm not sure. According to Alvin at the Historical Society, she would complain about a burglar getting into the nursery in the middle of the night once a week or so. Alvin would know," Dad said lowering the paper. "What has you so interested in the Millers?"

"Nothing, just curious. Did Mr. Green tell you what the burglar did in the nursery?" I asked, sure I already knew the answer.

"The story was odd, so I remember. The burglar did nothing. He just stood by the crib and watched the baby. The police investigated and there was no sign of forced entry or any evidence that someone had been there at all. Mr. Miller chalked the whole thing up to post-partum depression, which is," Dad said looking at me.

"I know what it is Dad."

Dad knew the drill by now; I would get something in my mind and would ride that train until it came to a complete stop.

"Mr. Green told you all that?" I asked.

"Yes, Mr. Green told me. He thought I'd like to know some interesting facts about the house at one of my first Historical Society meetings."

"What else did Mr. Green tell you?" I was sounding like a policeman on an interrogation but Dad was used to this.

"He said that Mrs. Miller started cracking up and wanted to move away. She moved back with her folks until Mr. Miller sold the house and found another one closer to his work."

"What did you think when you heard all of that?" I kept on with the interrogation.

"I felt bad for the Millers, especially Mr. Miller. And before you ask, No, I don't think that there was an intruder of some kind watching the baby at night," Dad answered. I could tell that I was starting to wear him out.

"What did the 'burglar' look like?" I asked.

"Really, son, how much longer are we going to do this?"

"Not much longer."

"The burglar was dressed in black with a white mask or something; I don't remember the details."

"Which room was the nursery?"

"Yours." This shouldn't have surprised me but it did. I changed direction.

"Did you ever hear of the Delmarre family?"

"I think they owned the house before the Millers but I'm not sure."

"Do you know anything about them?"

"Honestly, son, I don't and if Alvin told me I've since forgotten."

I stopped and registered all the data that Dad had given me. I was trying to determine if I had all the facts from him that he could give me. There was something else, the talisman.

"Have you ever found carved or painted stones in the yard?" I started.

"Stones, what do stones have to do with the Millers?" Dad was getting impatient.

"They are markers left behind by the Native Americans who used to live in this area," I countered.

"Yes, I know all about the Namtuxet Indians. No, I didn't find one mowing the lawn or something but I never looked. If anything was here, it was probably removed when the developer bought the land." Dad began to sound perturbed.

"They're not Indians, Dad, they're Native Americans. If you were to look for the stones, where would you look around here?" I was definitely asking one of the right guys. Dad had been involved in the Historical Society from the first month we moved here and was helping write an illustrated history of the town for publication.

Dad put down his paper and folded his arms and stared at me. I could see his mind working. "I guess I'd start at the end of the street where it meets West Street. I'd follow the stream that wanders behind our house, there's a thicket of trees there. I guess anywhere that the developers didn't plow into the ground, something could actually still be there."

"Thanks, Dad; I'm done." I gave him a slight smile to thank him for his effort.

"If you find one of those, don't move it; let me know first — OK?" He smiled back.

"Sure Dad," I agreed.

Then he said, "what's the connection with the Namtuxet and the previous owners?"

"I think that Mrs. Miller's intruder is still here," I said and walked away.

Chapter 15

J was in my pajamas and neatly tucked in bed by 9pm. My homework was done, teeth brushed and the lights were left on. The big flashlight was off as the battery had died; I replaced it with another from the garage but it was Dad's last one and I knew that the batteries were expensive. I needed it to last so it stayed on the nightstand in the 'off' position.

Dad came to my bedroom door. He peered in and said, "You can keep the flashlight if it helps you sleep."

"Thanks, Dad; it does help."

"Step, do you mind if I ask you something?"

"Sure Dad."

"What did you mean when you said Mrs. Miller's intruder was still around?"

I considered the pending psychological assessment ahead of me. Instead of telling him every detail of the 'Tony situation,' I thought that I'd diffuse the situation by pointing to a subject I knew would catch his attention.

"I don't want to seem overly dramatic Dad, but we could be sitting on a graveyard. I recently went to the Historical Society. Mr. Green told me all about the Namtuxet, and the stone markers they used for gravesites. From what I understand, there's a possibility their gravesites were disturbed when our house was built. I don't want to sound superstitious, but if there were markers here, and the developers moved them ..."

Dad stood at the doorway, rubbing his fingers together, so I knew I piqued his curiosity. "Well I don't know about ghosts of the Namtuxet running around son, but I must say, we might want to investigate this further," he said. His fingers continued to rub together while he stood there lost in his thoughts.

"I have an idea," he finally said.

"Sure, what is it?"

"I have plenty of time off saved up. Why don't I take the afternoon off tomorrow, and pick you up from school? Together, we can look for the Namtuxet markers if there are any." He seemed a little excited about it.

"Sure, Dad; I'd really like that," I said.

"Goodnight, kiddo. I love you," he said from the doorway. It was a rarity to hear that from him.

I soaked it in for a brief moment and answered, "I love you, too." With that Dad left.

That night sleep came easily, even with the lights on. Tony stayed away as planned.

****

Always true to his word, Dad picked me up the next day. Mom took the opportunity to do some shopping and pick out some books at the library so Dad and I had the house to ourselves for a while. When we pulled into the driveway, I felt some pangs of angst — Cadence was conspicuous in her absence.

Dad went upstairs and changed into jeans as did I. He put on some old boots and a sweatshirt; I wore sneakers and a white t-shirt. We met in the living room where he showed me his notebook. It was strapped together with a rubber band; and a sharpened pencil in the metal spiral held it bound. In it were notes from Historical Society meetings and other research he had been doing. For years, he'd been working on creating an illustrated history of the town.

"I have some notes from some documents I found. One was an early map of the Atkins' Farm. The map showed all of the known Namtuxet markers they found when they started to farm the land," he said as he while turned the pages of his book, covered in handwritten notes and sketches.

"How did they find all of those? There must be a dozen or more," I said.

"There were about 20 that were found."

"How did the Atkins Family find them?"

"Remember, they had to cut the trees right from their land to make the barn and the house. The cellar was dug by hand and the foundation was field stone carried by cart; pretty primitive compared to modern machinery."

There was a knock on the door, and I jumped. I hadn't realized how anxious I was. Dad got up and opened the door.

"Hello Cadence. How are you today?" Dad asked.

"Fine and you?" She politely answered.

"Very well, thank you. We were about to do some snooping around the neighborhood if you'd like to join us," Dad offered as he motioned for her to come in.

"Dad, Cadence and I were going to do this ourselves until you volunteered," I explained to him.

"Why didn't you tell me? I don't want to overstep my bounds, son."

"Dad, we definitely need you. We could use your expertise," I said, Cadence smiling and nodding her head. Hearing this seemed to make Dad really happy. He clapped his hands together, and called us over to the kitchen table.

Dad unrolled a hand-drawn map of the neighborhood. "I drew this up myself," he said.

We would start at the end of the street and follow the small stream that travelled under West Street and through several back yards. Dad knew the neighbors much better than I did and would have to talk us out of any trouble for trespassing.

We left the house and headed to the end of the street. We crossed West Street and into the tree line starting in back of the Mason's house. Once there I noticed several things; there were several well-worn paths through the trees and the woods were so thick that I could no longer see houses. I knew that we weren't that far away but I'd been unaware how undeveloped that area really was.

We stood by the stream that was on Dad's map; it was about four feet across and maybe two feet deep at its deepest point. The water rushed out of a water pipe that must have been installed during the development. The pipe was three feet in diameter and had no grating on it. I couldn't imagine how a child hasn't been stuck in it yet.

"When it rains, or there's any kind of storm or snow melt, this drainage pipe takes the runoff from all the streets in the neighborhood and directs it toward the Canoe River," Dad started, "I never understood why they called it the 'Canoe River,' A canoe would probably be bigger than the river."

"Think there are markers here?" Cadence asked, looking around.

"None on the map, but who knows?" he said. We followed the river deeper into the thick forest behind our houses and soon we found ourselves on a path that seemed to show evidence of frequent foot traffic.

"Dad, why are there so many paths in the woods? Do you think people still use them?"

"Well, maybe some people walk their dogs here."

"My father says paths were here when he was a kid; people used to cut through Atkins' Farm to come out here to party," Cadence added.

"Party?" I asked.

"Teenagers drinking and smoking and stuff," Cadence said.

We were reaching our property line and we stopped. There was a granite property marker placed by the developer when they were dividing the individual lots. About ten yards off the path near a group of old maple trees was a large stone bulging from the earth. I walked to it, crunching over old leaves and sticks. It was covered in moss but I noticed that it was perfectly round; like a ball.

I heard someone else crunching over to me as I knelt down and ran my hands over the stone. Even with the moss covering most of it I could see distinctive markings on the stone. I had found one of the Namtuxet markers. Cadence knelt next to me and traced the carvings with her finger, pulling off the moss. The image was a stick figured man with two arms too many and a swirly design over his head.

"Find something?" Dad asked as he joined us. He could see it as well and he busily began writing in his notebook. I stood up to see what he was writing; he had taken some notes and then pulled out a printed sheet of paper containing a detailed map drawing of our house and property. He marked the map where we and the Namtuxet marker were.

"Nice job." Dad said while patting my shoulder.

"Yeah, that's great." Cadence started, "Is this a talisman?"

"No, Cadence, I don't think that it's a talisman. It's a marker for something, though."

"What do you think it's for?" I asked still looking at the drawing.

"I'm not sure. It could be where they stored something, it could be a warning or a property boundary; it could even mark a gravesite."

"Gravesite – oh God; I certainly hope not," Cadence said worriedly.

"I wouldn't worry," Dad smiled at her.

We examined the marker for a little longer then walked back towards the path. We found our next marker about fifty yards down the path right next to it. This one was a cube with worn edges and corners. It was about three feet above ground and we weren't sure how much was underground, if any at all. The top seemed to have been carved by a great many people; certainly not only by the Namtuxet, if at all. There was some faded spray paint on it as well.

The carvings were on each of the sides and were all different. One was a triangle, one was three squiggly lines, the next was another swirly design and the last one, facing our house, was a man with two arms too many. Dad made notes and marked his map of the property; then we were off.

"Apparently the Namtuxet were excellent at masonry. The last marker was perfectly round; this one is a cube. I'm guessing the next one will be a pyramid," I said.

"They were fairly advanced for a primitive culture," Dad said.

We walked further but found no more markers along the trail. We had gone the length of our street and turned to go back. Dad's comment was a bit deflating even though it wasn't intended to be. "If there are more markers they could be just about anywhere in these woods."

"Why don't we concentrate the woods behind our property, Dad?" I suggested. After all, it was the only area that concerned me. So we traipsed back there, and soon were at our property line. We stopped.

"Cadence, I'll go straight in from here; you go down about fifty feet or so and head in from there. Dad, just pick a line and head through the trees to our house. Shout if you find something," I instructed.

"Okay, but you both must be very careful. There are pricker bushes and thorns in there as well."

"Sure Dad, no problem," I said and began walking into the woods.

I was walking the boundary between our neighbors, the Blanche's, and our yard. I had to navigate through thick trees and bushes where no one walked for a long time, if ever, which was why it was so slow-going. I wasn't in too far when I could see the roof of our house far off to my right. I glanced around, looking for Dad or Cadence, but I couldn't see them. And then I tripped on something.

It was a lump under a blanket of sticks and leaves. I stood and began to remove the sticks and leaves from the lump; I was bare-handed so it took some effort. The bottom leaves were wet and smelly; and when I moved them bugs ran for cover. But here was another stone; this one was low to the ground.

"Dad, hey Dad!" I yelled for my father. I heard his reply come from closer than I'd expected. I could see through the trees that Dad was with Cadence. He was writing in his notebook and she was excited; they had found another marker as well. Then Dad left Cadence where she was and headed for me. I got on my knees and tried to find the carvings with my fingers. I wiped away the dirt and again, there was the man with too many arms.

"Found a marker, kiddo? Cadence found another one, too." Dad was next to me, out of breath. He was in pretty good shape but he ran to get to me as quickly as he could. Tracing the markings with his fingers, he began his note taking. His diagram followed.

"Want to see what Cadence found?" He turned to go back without waiting for my answer. I followed close behind using the same path he forged to get to me. We were all already dirty and I had scratches on my hands and face. Cadence did too, but she and Dad must have traversed a real muddy patch because their shoes were covered in muck.

Near the markers Cadence had found was the dried riverbed of Canoe River. There hadn't been much rain in a while. Cadence had found a group of four stones, arranged side by side. Each one was about two feet long and had a singular marking: the man, the swirl, the squiggly lines and the triangle. I looked to Cadence who was very pleased with herself. Dad was consulting his notebook with a furrowed brow.

"Problem, Dad?"

"I'm looking at the diagram of our house and property and there seems to be some correlation between the stone markers and our yard," he said continuing to look at the paper.

"What is it?" Cadence asked.

Dad looked up. "It seems, my young explorers, that the stones form a circle around our house."

Chapter 16

Cadence, my father and I walked out of the woods and into our backyard. Following my father's lead, we went over to the wooden picnic table and sat down. Dad spread out his diagram and held it in place with one hand while he removed a drawing compass from his shirt pocket. I watched him open the compass and take a measurement by eye. He then put the pointed leg of the compass near the center of the diagram and used the pencil in the other leg of the compass to draw a circle.

Cadence and I tucked in to watch. The circle went around our house, through part of the Blanches' property then touched the street and back to the woods where it went through the markers we had found. The four markers we found seemed to be evenly spaced but there looked to be another four markers missing.

According to the drawing, one would be in the Blanche's yard near our boundary and another would be near the front curb. The other two would be in our side yard, adjacent to the Blanche's house. They were marked on the diagram with an X and sat perfectly on the circle. Dad removed the compass, put it back in his pocket, and pushed the paper towards us. Cadence and I looked at the drawing and I noticed something very unusual.

"Hey, Dad, look at your diagram," I said as he stood. He looked at it, tracing the circle with his finger.

"Yeah, what am I looking at?" he said, and both he and Cadence looked at me instead of the map.

"The hole from the compass is the center of the circle and the center-point is basically in my room." I looked again at the diagram and the outline of our house. There was a small hole where my bedroom would be.

Dad took the map and looked up to the house. "So it is," he said nervously. He looked to me then to Cadence.

"Hold on a minute," he said, heading for the shed. He slid the metal door open, reached in and pulled out a long-handled shovel. Examining his map, with his shovel in hand, Dad looked like a pirate. He went to the front of the house and we followed.

He stood on the grass between the sidewalk and the curb and seemed to be calculating something. He motioned Cadence over as she was closest and gave her the map. He began to dig.

In about five minutes he was two feet down when the shovel made a loud *clang* as it struck something. Dad spent the next ten minutes making the hole wider. He was already dirty and sweating and he removed his sweatshirt. Underneath, he was wearing a blue t-shirt with a picture of Richard Nixon and the words 'Tricky Dick in 1980' on it. I couldn't understand my father's sense of humor.

I felt a little irresponsible with Dad doing all the work while we watched, but I did nothing to stop it. Dad stopped on his own accord, spiking the shovel into the sod. He took a moment to catch his breath then took the notebook from Cadence. We went to the hole to have a look.

At the bottom, in clear sight, was a cube just like the one along the pathway in back. It had the swirl carved into the top but that was all we could see. Dad had cleared the edges and then some, but the stone was too large to excavate in such a short time by hand.

"Could you go in the house and get us something to drink?" Dad asked.

"I'll go with you," Cadence offered. We went to the front door but she realized that she was too muddy to go in. I wiped my shoes on the mat and went into the house while Cadence waited on the porch. I grabbed a pitcher of Tang from the refrigerator and several Dixie cups then headed back outside.

Cadence followed me back to the hole by the street where Dad took several servings of Tang with big gulps. Then he said, "Follow me." We walked to the side yard where the next marker should have been. Dad began to dig but allowed me to take turns with him. This one took twenty minutes. After that, we were off to the next one, which took even longer. The Tang was gone and we were all dirty, Cadence just from standing there watching us. The last one was in the Blanches' yard. Dad would have to speak to Mr. Blanche to get permission to dig that one up.

We followed Dad to the back yard where he returned the shovel to the shed. We almost crumpled onto the picnic table. Cadence spoke first.

"Do you know what those markings mean?" she asked my Dad.

"I'm not sure. I think one is the sun — the swirly one. I think that the three squiggly lines mean water or a river. I don't know about the triangle and I've never seen the stick figure with four arms before," he answered. "I'm going to have to get Alvin out here to look at these. I drew the symbols in my notebook so maybe he'll be able to do some research on them for me."

"Do you think that it's a coincidence that the center of the circle is your bedroom?" Cadence asked, looking to me. I'd been hoping it was coincidence but was pretty sure that it wasn't.

"No, I don't think it's a coincidence at all," I said. Dad looked at me and I could see that his mind was working again.

"You said that you saw the Miller's intruder?" he asked. I still hadn't given him the entire story, only bits and pieces.

"Yes." I admitted.

"Black clothes and white mask?" he asked again.

"Yes," I said again.

"I want you to show me. I'm going to sleep in your room tonight. This way I won't miss anything," he said.

"That might not be the best idea," I began.

"I can't imagine why. If there's nothing to it then no harm done. If there is something, well..." Dad trailed off.

"Then I won't be going to Dr. Erkahn for long," I finished for him. He smiled a little at that.

"Right," he said.

Cadence stayed a while longer then went home for supper. We went into the house, kicking our shoes off at the door. Dad called Mr. Green on the telephone but the conversation was brief. Dad asked Mr. Green to come by the house, that he had something important to show him.

"That will do," Dad signed off and hung up the phone.

"What?" I asked.

"Mr. Green will be here tomorrow. He's going to have Mr. Topaz come along with him," Dad said. "Let's you and I get cleaned up and get some dinner."

We both washed up, and before he started cooking, I requested omelets, one of his better dishes, and he obliged. Mom pulled into the driveway just as I was setting the table.

"Have a nice afternoon?" Dad asked from the stove as Mom came in.

"Wonderful. I picked out new curtains; I made my dentist appointment; I signed out two books from the library; and I got a car wash," Mom said as she went to Dad for a kiss. "What did you boys do? Get into any trouble?" If she only knew.

"Cadence came over and the three of us hung around outside," Dad answered. I looked at him, surprised.

Mom put her things away then returned to the kitchen. "Seeing a lot of Cadence, aren't you?" Mom asked.

I didn't answer; I was busy drinking my milk. I knew she could tell that I wasn't feeling talkative and so she dropped the conversation right there. But Dad was still available so she turned to him. "Fondue tonight?"

"Omelets, a special request from the young lord," Dad said. "Dinner is served."

****

Dad must have explained things fairly well to Mom because he came to bed with me at 9 o'clock on the nose. I had already said goodnight to Mom. My teeth were brushed and I was in bed. I was a bit nervous that Dad would soon find out about the hole in the bed; my saving grace was that the hole would be insignificant compared to meeting Tony.

Dad turned out the lights and hopped into my full size bed. It had been Dad and Mom's bed, but they purchased a new waterbed, I inherited it from them. Dad didn't seem to notice the hole so I didn't mention it. I was on the side with the nightstand and had checked the flashlight before Dad arrived. He left the door wide open so the bathroom light bled into the room.

It had been quite some time since Dad and I had gone camping. When I was younger Dad and I would sleep in the living room like Manny and I did. We would pretend that we were camping outside, which Dad thought was good fun. I would miss my comfortable bed a flight of stairs away but I always played along just to make him happy.

We said goodnight but I was prepared for an interesting evening of fun and frolic and was sure Dad would be very frightened. It was up to Tony now to come for his regular visit, although none of his visits were very 'regular' anymore.

Sleep came for both of us. But, once again, Tony did not disappoint.

Chapter 17

The banging had begun. I looked at the digital clock and it was 2:15am. I sat up and grabbed the flashlight careful not to turn it on. Then I nudged Dad, who was on his side and breathing deeply. He didn't move so I nudged him again.

The bed jolting woke Dad up. Dad rolled over to me to see what I wanted, but I pointed to the foot of the bed as it jolted again. The second jolt removed any lingering sleep Dad was feeling, he sat upright. I could see the outline of his face in the dim light and barely make out his eyes; they were opened wide.

"MMMMMYYYYYYYOOOOOOOOOOOOOOOOOOOOOMM MMMMMMMM"

Tony growled as he pulled himself out from under the bed. He was pulling the covers from us as he clawed his way out. His luminescent face glowed above the bed as he rose.

"MMMMMYYYYYYYOOOOOOOOOOOOOOOOOOOOOMM MMMMMMMM"

That time he revealed his mouthful of teeth. I looked to Dad who was petrified still and said incredulously, "You never heard him before from your room?" Dad's face remained locked on Tony.

"MMMYYY RRROOOOOOMMM"

Then I knew. Tony was telling us that we were in his room.

I tried to talk to him. "Anthony Delmarre, this was once your room. Why have you come back?"

"My Room."

Tony's voice was gravely and deep but it had quickly become coherent. Tony remained at the foot of the bed so I felt safe taking the opportunity to further the conversation.

"You *are* Anthony Delmarre. You *died* when you were eight years old. Your parents sold this house and moved away. Why have you come back?" I said.

Tony darted down towards me and stared at me, nose to nose.

"*My Room,*" he said, but it sounded almost like a question. Dad finally broke from his paralysis and pushed Tony away from me. Tony moved like a tethered balloon.

Dad stood beside the bed in a position that looked prepared for an attack.

Tony resumed his position at the end of the bed and said, "*Thisss izzz mmmy rrroooommm.*"

Then Dad spoke, "No, this is my son's room! This is our house!"

Tony roared, "*MMMYYY RRROOOOOOMMM!!!*" and darted after my Dad. I feared that Tony would claw my Dad so I did the only thing I could. I turned on the powerful flashlight and Tony disappeared with a 'pop' like a balloon bursting. Dad was standing next to the bed with his back against the wall. He looked terrified.

The sound of Mom opening the bedroom door and marching down the hall brought us back to reality. I turned on the overhead light and looked at Dad up against the wall.

Mom came to the door and said, "What are you guys doing? What's all the noise?"

I looked at Mom and then Dad and said, "That was Tony."

****

Mom finally went back to bed after Dad assured her everything was alright. He didn't *look* like everything was alright but Mom bought what he was selling and returned to bed. He looked to me and said, "Alright, I want every detail."

I sat on my desk chair and he sat on the bed and I told him everything that I knew. Tony started visiting when I was eight years old, I said. He had never done anything before but float and stare at me. The physical manifestations were more a recent thing and Tony had become clearer to me. I told Dad about the article on Anthony Delmarre and my visit with both Mr. Green and Mr. Topaz. I told him about the flashlight and the video tape and about Manny's night terrors. I told him about Cadence.

"I tried telling you this stuff before," I said.

"I guess I heard you but just didn't *listen*," Dad admitted.

"Now I don't need Dr. Erkahn, right?" I asked. Dad was still shaken but much calmer than a short time before.

"I'll talk with your mother about that. We'll see." He tried to smile.

"What was he like?" I asked.

"What was who like?" Dad seemed confused.

"When you were protecting me you *touched* Tony. What was that like?" I said still excited.

"Oh yeah, I touched his cloak; it felt like satin; definitely satin. Underneath was firm but not hard, like there was a person in there," he explained.

"I think that there was," I said.

Dad stood up and began to pace. "You're convinced it's Anthony; I'm convinced that those Namtuxet markers have something to do with this. Neither one of us can put it together so I'm taking tomorrow off. I'm too excited to sleep; I'm too excited to do anything and I haven't taken a day off in several months until today. I'm going to stay home again tomorrow and have Alvin come by while you're at school and help me figure out the markers."

He looked around the room once more; he checked the closet and under the bed, still not convinced that everything was fine. "You want to sleep somewhere else tonight?" he asked concerned.

"No, I'll keep the lights on. I don't think he'll be back tonight," I said.

"I'll be downstairs looking at my notes if you need me," he said then kissed my forehead.

"OK, Dad; I'll see you in the morning." I smiled back at him. He left. Now that Dad and Mom knew, I feel relieved, and I had no problem falling back to sleep.

****

I awoke on my own; my internal alarm clock never failed. I dressed and went downstairs. I could hear Mom in the shower as I descended the stairs. In the living room Dad was asleep on the couch; his notes and papers scattered about. He was snoring loudly and he was sleeping in an awkward position that I knew he'd feel for most of the day.

I ate my cereal with the sounds of Dad in the background. I was ready for school when Mom came downstairs.

"Looks like your father had a rough night," she said, looking over at him.

"You could say that,"

She looked at me suspiciously so I added, "He told me that he was taking another day off from work."

"I don't know what you two are up to but I'm sure it's a doozy," Mom said as she headed to the kitchen. Several minutes later we were on our way to school.

Chapter 18

After school, Mom and I pulled into the driveway behind Dad's Lincoln. Mr. Green's Aries K car was parked out front. The car was green and the interior was green. Mr. Green really must have liked green.

Dad was in the front yard with Mr. Green and Mr. Topaz peering into the hole next to the street. The three men were dressed for hiking and had mud on their shoes and dirt on their pants. Mom and I went over to see what was going on. The men were consulting the map with the circle and the markers and speaking excitedly.

"Hello, gentlemen," Mom addressed all of them.

"Hi sweetheart," Dad said as he leaned in for a kiss.

"Spent your day off with these troublemakers?" she asked playfully. Mr. Green and Mr. Topaz blushed. She looked to the ground. "What's with the hole in the front yard?"

"These are the markers left on our property by the Namtuxet that I told you about. This grouping forms a perfect circle around our house," Dad explained. Mom looked from the hole to Dad and back at the hole. Dad acquiesced, "We'll fill it in when we're done. It may be a couple of days."

"Well," she said thoughtfully, "you should put something over it so no one trips and breaks their neck." She turned and went into the house.

"Hi Dad, Hello Mr. Green, Mr. Topaz," I said, addressing all three.

"Hey Step, I showed Mr. Green and Mr. Topaz the stones in the woods. Mr. Green thinks he knows what these are," Dad said as excited as a kid on Christmas morning.

"What are they?" I asked.

"This is a holy ground for the Namtuxet, my boy. It's quite a great find and I understand that you were the person responsible for finding them," Mr. Green said.

"Dad and Cadence helped quite a bit," I said.

"Yes, well, I'm sure you'd like to know that the eight stone markers encompass this sacred holy ground and it is guarded by those who had gained the Namtuxet's highest honor." Mr. Green was trying to sound very worldly to me. I noticed Mr. Topaz rolling his eyes.

"What made this ground so holy to them?" I prodded trying to move Mr. Green along.

"This ground, they believe, acts a portal to their afterlife. It's a doorway to heaven, where they and their ancestors had passed through for countless generations, if you'd like." Mr. Green spread his arms and smiled wide.

"What about the markers themselves, do they do anything?" I was drawn to the idea.

"No, the markers are here for the living. They mark the holy place and may also mark those who guard it," he answered.

"Like headstones?" I asked.

"Possibly," Dad said.

"So there could be bodies somewhere around those rocks, including this one right in our front yard?" I said a little too loudly. I was shushed by my father.

"It's possible but I'm not sure," Mr. Green said.

"He doesn't know anything," Mr. Topaz said grinning.

"Please keep this between us for the time being. We don't want anyone getting alarmed about the possibility of human remains in our neighborhood," Dad said to Mr. Green and Mr. Topaz, as much as to me.

"You don't want Mom to know because she'll be upset."

Dad shrugged his shoulders but shook his head up and down.

"Apparently the developers didn't look too hard for evidence of the Namtuxet after all. I'm sure it was easier to just plow it under if they found something," Mr. Topaz added.

I looked up the street and could see Cadence heading our way on her bicycle. She was coming from Manny's house. I remembered that I hadn't spoken to Manny in a few days and I should make an effort to do so. Cadence rode up to us and rested her bike on its side. All four of us greeted her simultaneously. She smiled and gave a little wave.

"You got here in time, Cadence. Mr. Green was telling us about the stones," I said looking into her eyes. I didn't even notice what she was wearing.

"Really? That's so exciting," she said trying to sound grown-up but I could hear her voice shake.

"The eight stones mark a holy ground for the Namtuxet and there may be bodies buried under them." I teased her. She narrowed her eyes at me. She was obviously nervous about them and about our house.

"Cadence thinks that the stones might be dangerous. Do you know what the carvings mean?" I asked Mr. Green.

"I think so. Your father correctly guessed that the three 'S' shaped lines represent water. He also guessed that the 'swirl' as you put it, represents the sun, but I believe that it represents the air. I also believe that the triangle represents fire. Together they represent three of the main elements: air, fire and water. The fourth, Earth, is represented by the circle that the markers have formed," he said.

"What about the man with four arms?" I asked.

"He represents the guardian buried there to protect the holy space," Mr. Green said.

"Then why does he have four arms, Alvin?" Mr. Topaz interrupted.

"Because, Bill, he doesn't have four arms, he only has two arms. What they have drawn represents motion; the man is moving his arms up and down," Mr. Green said smugly.

"Why would he need to move his arms up and down?"

"For flight dear Bill; he flies to the spirit world."

"That's a guess on your part. The guy flaps his arms and flies? That's a laugh! Alvin, you have no idea what you're talking about."

Mr. Green shook his head and looked to the rest of us. "I have been in this town my whole life other than my time away at college," he started, and then he turned to Mr. Topaz, "to *earn my master's degree*! Unlike some other Neanderthals, I have studied the Namtuxet most of my life. I have many books and journals on them including some first-hand accounts from their descendants as well as from townspeople who dealt with them on a regular basis."

There was a pause when I asked, "Where are those descendants now?"

"The Namtuxet way of life is gone, young sir, but the people didn't completely die out. Some interbred with the European settlers or they moved on and merged with other 'Indian' Nations."

Dad had been conspicuously quiet during all of the banter but he got down to the meat of the matter. "Could this portal actually open and let, oh...I dunno...spirits into our world?"

"I suppose that would be a matter of faith and no more unrealistic as the Rapture or any other of our beliefs," Mr. Green answered, with his eyes on Mr. Topaz the whole time. "Besides, the eight guardians are supposed to stop that from happening."

"Who are these eight guardians?" Cadence asked.

"Chiefs, medicine men, priests, warriors; those who were considered worthy by their words and their deeds," Mr. Green sighed. He was older and getting tired of the excitement.

"Were they, uh, sacrificed here, Mr. Green?" Cadence asked worriedly.

"No, child, I think they became guardians and were placed here *after* they had expired naturally. I'm sure the Namtuxet wouldn't have wanted any angry guardians," he said, comforting her. He looked to Mr. Topaz and added, "I'm getting tired and need to rest; this excitement is a bit much for me. We'll be by this weekend with the video camera and film the excavation of the stone in the front yard."

"Mom will not like that," I said to anyone who would listen.

"It's for the book we're doing. We'll fill in the hole afterwards," Mr. Topaz said, and then he shook everyone's hand, including mine, and started walking towards his car. Mr. Green did the same, but more slowly, then got into his car with some effort and drove off. Dad went into the house, leaving Cadence and me out front by the hole.

As soon as they left, I told her about Tony's latest visit.

Chapter 19

$\mathcal{T}$hat whole evening Dad could barely contain his excitement though he did his best to hide his fear. He was afraid of the house, of my room, of the night and of the dark; and he said so. This was countered with the joy at the discovery in our yard which could have national implications in the anthropological world in which Dad lived. The illustrated history of our town had been his baby for almost two years and was nearing completion. The discovery of the Namtuxet markers threw a monkey wrench into any time table that he and the Historical Society had adhered to.

I, on the other hand, tried my best to keep to my schedule. My homework was done; my teeth brushed; and, I was in my pajamas before nine. I said my goodnights and went to my room for my own nighttime ritual of checking the closet, under the bed and the big flashlight on the end table. I again kept the lights on and got into bed. The handmade blanket from Grandma had been working to cover the hole in my bed splendidly up to that point but I no longer feared discovery. Dad was a converted believer. I read for a while then put the book down.

Sleep still came easily for me and for that I was grateful.

****

I awoke to a banging noise and muffled voices. I looked to the clock and it was six am; the noises were coming from downstairs. I rose and shuffled to the staircase then descended. Dad was again asleep on the couch; the television was playing an old Jimmy Cagney movie. Every light on the first floor was illuminated. I looked at my father with a three-day growth of beard sleeping in the fetal position and decided to try and wake him.

I pushed him by the shoulder but he didn't wake up. I tried again and this time he sat bolt upright with eyes wide. "What's happening? What's going on?" he asked wildly.

"It's morning, Dad. Are you working today?" I asked. He looked at me but didn't appear to recognize me.

"What day is this?" he said starting to blink.

"Friday," I said, and I shook my head at him like he'd lost his marbles. I left him to go get a bowl of cereal. This was off routine for me, as I usually dressed and made my bed first, but I was throwing caution to the wind and eating first instead.

Dad staggered into the kitchen then grabbed a bowl and spoon. He joined me at the table. I could see in his eyes that the blankness about him was gone.

"I stayed up too late," he said as he poured the milk onto the cereal.

"Yes, I'm sure," was all I could add.

He took a bite and looked at me; he watched me eat for a while. He finally asked, "Did our friend under the bed come last night?"

"No. I think the lights scare him off." I knew I told him that before. He seemed to relax a little and ate more heartily.

"You guys are going to film yourselves digging up the Namtuxet marker out front?" I asked.

"Yeah; the guys from the high school Audio/Video club are going to do it for us tomorrow. They'll get credit and we'll get a copy of the final edit. I plan on sending it to some of our contacts to see if it could get picked up by PBS or something," Dad said in between bites.

"What about the marker in the Blanches' yard?" I asked.

"We'll do that one the following weekend, weather permitting. I'm heading to the Historical Society museum for our meeting after work tonight so I won't be home for supper."

I finished and put my dishes in the sink then headed upstairs to complete the first half of my routine.

****

Cadence was waiting for me after school and Mom invited her into the house. We ate cookies and milk at the kitchen table.

"I am going to get my hair done in a little while and then I have to go to the nursing home because it's my volunteer night," Mom said as she walked past us through the kitchen. "Your father's going to the Historical Society tonight after work so I made lasagna last night and it's in the freezer," she said, poking her head back in, after changing her shirt. "All you have to do is warm it up," she said, after changing her shoes in the hallway. "I should be home by eight at the latest," she said as she grabbed her coat and headed toward the door.

She returned and continued, "Cadence, you can stay for dinner if it's OK with your folks, but you should go home after that."

She came over and kissed my cheek, then Cadence's. Cadence was not prepared and tried to back away. Mom didn't notice and said goodbye as she went out the door. The Volvo fired up and she was off. Cadence and I looked at each other as we finished our cookies. I shrugged as if to say, "I have no idea."

We went to the living room couch and I turned on the television with the remote control. My family was not a television family; we rarely watched it. Instead, we read; all of us read. Dad liked the papers and periodicals as well as a novel here and there; Mom read her classics; and, I enjoyed everything else. I flipped through the channels but found nothing so I turned it off.

"How's Manny these days?" I asked trying to make conversation.

"He's doing better. He says he wants you to come visit him if you want to."

"Sure, maybe the two of us could go together sometime tomorrow."

"I'd like that; I'm sure Manny would as well. Isn't tomorrow the day your Dad's going to dig up the marker out front?"

"Yes, he has the guys from the high school Audio/Video department filming it."

Cadence and I locked eyes. I searched hers not knowing what to say next. I had so many things to tell her but I could think of nothing to say. Her eyes were looking at mine from one to the other. My feelings for her had blossomed but I had no idea how to deal with it. I wondered if she felt as flustered as I did. I also wondered if she had similar feelings for Manny.

Then we both heard a noise coming from upstairs. It sounded like crying from a young child. It grew louder so I stood to investigate; Cadence stood up as well. I looked to her and put one finger to my lips telling her to be quiet then led her up the stairs. We stopped at the top landing and looked into my room. The crying continued.

There was a small boy standing at the foot of my bed with his face buried in his hands. He wore jeans, canvas sneakers and a black satin cape. I could see that he was wearing a mask; it was the type with the elastic that went around the back of the head to keep it in place. Out from the top was a thick mop of brown hair.

Slowly, Cadence and I entered the room. The boy had his back to us and was sobbing heavily. Cadence went to him; she knelt beside him and touched his shoulder. "Are you OK little boy?" she asked.

The little boy looked up from his hands and turned; and there was no monster, just poor little Anthony Delmarre, lost, scared and crying.

"My r-r-room?" was all he could say; this caused another wave of sobbing. He hugged Cadence and she hugged him back. I stood back and watched this with some trepidation. Tony was a prankster and had done some outrageous things lately.

I was flooded with emotion as I watched the little boy. I was confused and scared — I thought Tony would only come at night and was afraid of the light. Was Tony going to trick us and hurt Cadence? But I was sad too; Anthony was so scared and alone. And, I was falling in love; Cadence was so tender and caring. I rarely felt much emotion and was having a hard time with the waves of them crashing down on me. I wanted to run.

Instead, I remained and tried to assess the situation to find a resolution. I would handle this as logically as possible. I knelt down next to Cadence and Anthony put one arm around my neck; his head was between Cadence's and my own. With my left hand I gently rubbed his back; I remembered my mother doing the same for me when I was little. The sobbing abated after a while.

"Isn't this my room anymore?" Anthony asked me, tears still in his eyes.

"I'm sorry, Anthony, but this is our house. We bought it several years ago," I told him.

He appeared to have accepted the answer. "Where are my Mommy and Daddy?" he said, trying not to cry.

"We'll find them for you, sweetie," Cadence said. I looked to her and gave her a pained expression. She knew the circumstances well enough not to promise anything.

"OK, Cadence. Thank you," Anthony said.

"You know her name?" I asked him.

"Yes, and I know yours, too," he said. I let go of him and stood. I grabbed the box of tissues from the dresser and gave him one. Cadence helped him remove the mask so that he could blow his nose. Anthony Delmarre was a cute kid with big, brown eyes.

I decided to strike while the iron was hot. "Why were you under my bed and in my closet, Anthony?"

"I was trying to scare you away but you just won't leave. I want my room back," he said, chin trembling.

"But Anthony, you visited me for years and did nothing. It was only recently that you started knocking things over, scratching things or talking to me," I said as I sat him down on the bed. I sat on one side of him and Cadence sat on the other.

He thought for a moment but looked confused. "Years? I haven't been here *that* long. I made the baby leave but then you were here. At first I couldn't talk but you saw me and talked to me. I got real mad because you wouldn't leave. Then I got strong enough to talk to you. I thought you were a bully," he said, sad but defiant. Cadence helped him blow his nose again and wipe his face; he had regained his composure. "The *Others* taught me to get strong, taught me how to talk to you."

"Others? What others Anthony? Who are the others?" Cadence asked.

"They are here, in the yard. They are from the before time," he whispered.

"The before time?" she asked.

"Yeah, before the house and the street; *they* were here," he said.

"What did they look like, Anthony?" I asked. He had to think for a moment.

"Like Indians on television. They don't ride horses, though. They live in stick houses and hunt animals and grow corn and other stuff." He was getting stronger, less afraid.

"Tell me how they taught you to get strong, to talk to me," I said.

He thought again. "I don't know; they make pictures in my head. They can talk to me in my head, too — like radio. They don't talk to the people in the grass, though. They don't trust those people."

"Tell me about the people in the grass," I pushed.

"Most of them look like us and talk like us. I talked to them and those people aren't scary, they're just lost — like me."

"How many people are there, Anthony? How many Others?"

"There are *lots* of them."

Chapter 20

I looked at the little boy sitting on the bed next to me who was as real and solid as I was. I didn't realize that he had taken my hand, while Cadence held onto his other one. With my free hand, I was holding a white rubber mask similar to the one Lon Chaney wore to cover his character's hideous face in the old silent movie, *Phantom of the Opera*.

I saw the movie years before with my father at the Star Theater, the small local cinema in the center of town. They said that inside was decorated just like the Grauman's Chinese Theatre in California. Once a month they would play classic films.

"Anthony, how are you here during the daytime? Don't the lights frighten you?" I asked him, putting the mask down on the bed.

"No, I gave up trying to scare you at night. I used to get scared of the dark so I thought that you would, too. I like the light better," he answered.

"Is there light where the Others are?" Cadence asked.

"Oh, yes; they are outside and it's sunny a lot of the time." Anthony looked to her then to me. "Would you like to see the Others?"

Cadence and I looked to each other over Anthony's head; we had a conversation with our facial expressions. Cadence looked worried.

"I'll go with you, Anthony," I said to him. Then I said to Cadence, "You don't have to go if you don't want to."

"Where is it that we're going, Anthony?" she asked. I also looked to Anthony for the answer.

"To the Others, Cadence. You can call me Tony, it's alright," Anthony said, letting go of our hands and standing. He continued, "It's not exactly *where* we are going; it's kinda like *when*."

"I'll go with you," Cadence said to me, I smiled at that. Part of me was frightened for her safety but the rest of me doubted any danger. I thought I would ask anyway.

"Is that place dangerous? How do we get there?" I asked looking into his drying eyes.

"We can go through there," Anthony said, as he pointed to the closet. "You should be safe."

"We *should* be safe." I repeated emphasizing the *should.*

Tony went to the closet door and opened it. In it I could see my clothes hanging from the rod, my games on the shelf up high and assorted shoes neatly arranged along the back. There would barely be enough room for the three of us in there. Tony stepped in, I followed, and Cadence was last. She took my hand. I took Tony's hand and he said, "Close the door."

****

As soon as Cadence closed the door, the closet was pitch black. Cadence added to the tension by saying to no one in particular, "I can't believe that we're doing this."

I felt a gentle breeze and could smell the outdoors; there was grass and pine. Then I heard the sound of a stream or a brook bubbling. Cadence must have heard it too because she squeezed my hand harder. The darkness began to lift slowly. As I looked up, I saw the circle of the sun. It was faded as if I was wearing ten pairs of sunglasses on top of each other.

But the brightness grew, and soon there was an outline of trees. The sky became a deep, purple-blue and I could start to make out clouds. It was like Grandma's old television set before she broke down and bought a new one. When I turned it on, a dot would appear in the center of the screen and, as the tubes warmed up, the image would grow and brighten.

The light reached its full potential and we found ourselves standing outside in grass that reached our knees. From a line of trees not far away, the sound of the stream was coming. I turned around and saw one of the Namtuxet markers we had found a few dozen yards away. Tony let go of our hands.

"This is our yard long ago!" Tony said and ran off towards the trees. Cadence let go of my hand and we instinctively took off after Tony. At the edge of the tree line was another stone marker. It was a very short walk to the stream and the path that ran alongside it. It definitely looked similar to the path behind our house but was wider and somehow, the trees looked different.

Tony stopped at the stream and drank from his cupped hands. The stream was almost twenty feet across but only a few feet deep at the most. A fallen tree across it made a bridge to the other side. The water was crystal clear and moved at a quick pace. Cadence knelt down and put her hand in the water; she pulled it out immediately, saying, "It's cold!"

Tony stopped and watched us taste the water; it was clean and tasted marvelous. We stood and Tony joined us. "The Others should be somewhere around here," he said, scanning the area. Then he cupped his mouth with his hands and yelled, "They are safe. Please come out!"

Cadence tensed then took my hand again. I was nervous and squeezed back. We scanned the area with Tony.

"What's happening?" Cadence asked nervously.

"I think that they are looking you over. Don't worry, they'll come out soon," Tony said still looking around. I tried not to look worried but was starting to feel that way.

There was a rustle in the woods, then the snap of a breaking stick; we turned. From behind a tree came what I surmised to be a Namtuxet native. He wore leggings and a leather tunic, probably made from deerskin; his moccasins reached to his thigh. He wore his black hair long and a headband of beads. Over his shoulder, he carried a woven bag like a large purse. He had no noticeable weapons.

"That's the Fire Chief. He's their leader," Tony told us. I was unsure if it meant that he put out fires or started them; possibly both. The Fire Chief walked up to Tony and picked him up in his arms. He smiled and gave the boy a hug. I could see Cadence relax just a little.

He put Tony down then walked up to me. He wasn't a particularly tall man but was still several inches taller than me. He was lean and muscular but his face was friendly. He didn't speak, as he stood before me, but he put one hand on my shoulders and suddenly I knew more. His touch was like a mild electrical shock, and in it was transference of information between us. I could feel his presence in my mind.

I no longer felt that we were in danger. The Fire Chief looked to Cadence and then ran his index finger along the outline of her face. He stepped back and bowed slightly to her. The Fire Chief then turned and walked back into the woods.

"He is a guardian," I said aloud, mostly out of amazement.

"I know; I could feel him in my head," Cadence said. I looked to her for a moment puzzled, and then I realized that we had been holding hands the whole time. Somehow the transference travelled to her through me.

"I think that the Fire Chief just wanted to get to know you," Anthony added.

"Is that how they communicate with you, Anthony?" Cadence asked.

"Yeah, mostly; sometimes they show me pictures," he said, taking her hand. "Let's go see Mr. Joe. He talks to them too." He led us through the stream to the fields beyond.

Chapter 21

*W*ith Tony in the lead, we walked but we were not tired from the exercise. We left the outcrop of trees and stayed out of the tall grass. There was a beaten path that was not very wide. It wasn't long before we reached a meadow filled with blooming wildflowers. In the short grass of a small hill, sat what looked to be a couple dozen people, men and women both.

The people in the grass were mostly all Caucasian although I did see an Asian man sitting among them. They were sitting in groups; some were talking, some were napping and others seemed to be enjoying themselves, just taking in the scenery. A few had a long straw of grass sticking out of their mouth. Tony stopped; they seemed to notice us looking at them.

"Those are the people in the grass," Tony said. "The Indians stay away from them most of the time. I don't think that they like them."

"They probably don't trust them," I said.

"Why is that?" Cadence asked.

"History, Cadence; they're European colonists. They stole the land from the native people. I wouldn't trust them either if I were one of the Namtuxet," I explained.

"They're not so bad – really. I like talking to them," Tony looked at me.

"Look at their clothes," Cadence added. She was right; the collection of clothing had been in style at one point or another but in the distant past. Only a handful wore items from the same point in history. Two men wore the triangular hat from the time of the nation's birth; some others wore items from the industrial revolution of the 1800s. A few wore suits and hats from the early part of the twentieth century. The women's dresses reflected the same time periods.

"Notice anything else, Cadence?" I asked. She hesitated a moment and then turned to me.

"No children," I said. Though some of the people appeared very young no one sitting on the hill was prepubescent. Aside from Cadence and me, Tony was the youngest in the place. "Why are there no kids, Tony?"

"I don't know; I wish there was someone to play with," Tony started, "the Fire Chief says that the people on the hill don't belong here."

"Where do they belong?" Cadence looked from the hill to Tony.

"In heaven, I guess. I don't really know," Tony said shrugging his shoulders. "Help me look for Mr. Joe."

"Who's Mr. Joe?" I asked, looking again at the people on the hill.

"He's the brown man. He's my friend!" Tony's face lit up with a smile.

"Is he black, Tony?" I smiled back.

"Well, he's more of a brown; he's the only brown man here. He talks to the Chiefs sometimes; they trust him. The people on the hill don't really know what's going on but Mr. Joe does. He told me that they're lost but for lost folks they don't really seem to be doing much about finding their way home," Tony said and started walking again.

Off in the distance, a black man wearing a brown three-piece suit and a fedora with a snap brim, walked towards us. I could hear him whistling. He was older, his face covered with deep lines, but his stature and his gait spoke of someone much younger. Tony broke off in a run to greet him.

"Mr. Joe, Mr. Joe!" Tony cried out.

"Hey there little man!" Mr. Joe cried back. Tony ran to him and Mr. Joe scooped him up in a big hug. "Who have you brought with you, there?"

"These are my friends from the other side, Joe," Tony said. Mr. Joe carried Tony over to us, put Tony down, and then held out his hand. Cadence held and shook it. I held my hand out to him, waiting for him to shake my hand as well. I smiled when he took my hand. He had a firm handshake. I looked down and noticed Mr. Joe was wearing two-toned leather Oxfords.

"Good day to you. I am Roosevelt Joseph at your service. My friends call me 'Little Joe'."

Joe removed his hat and bowed slightly. "Little Tony here calls me 'Mr. Joe' so that'd work as well. You two can call me Joe." His smile was wide and genuine. One of his teeth was gold, and conspicuously placed in the upper front. 'Little Joe' must have been a play on words because he was over six feet tall and thin as a rail.

"How do you do, Mr. Joe," Cadence said as cordially as she could.

"Fine, little lady, just fine," Mr. Joe replied. Tony was standing next to him holding his hand and looking up at the conversation.

"I see that little Tony finally got you two to come over for a visit." Joe motioned with his free hand to the landscape around us.

"Where exactly is here, Mr. Joe?" I asked.

"Oh, that's not such an easy question to answer," Mr. Joe began as he tipped his hat back on his head. "I think that this is a way station of sorts, a spot kind of in between, if you catch my drift."

"Not exactly, sir," I replied.

"Now people called my father 'sir.' You just call me Joe." He smiled and winked to Cadence. "Let's walk and talk. I've got business to attend to."

"What kind of business, Mr. Joe?" Tony said.

"I'm looking for the statues again, Tony. Want to help?" Mr. Joe said.

"What are the statues?" Cadence asked Joe while walking.

"The statues are people, Cadence." Joe stopped walking and looked at her. "They are people just like you and me; they just can't believe that they're dead. So they stand there for a long while just staring at the ground."

"Dead?" Cadence was a bit alarmed.

"Sweet child, don't you know everyone here is already dead? We have passed on," Joe said and started walking again. "Every one of us except you two," he added.

Cadence was absorbing that information.

"So what do you do with the statues?" I asked.

"I try to get them to move on, to go with the rest of the folks sitting on the hill," Joe answered. "I try to collect them all in one place."

"Why?" I asked.

"Because, we have to hope, eventually we will all be going home." He smiled.

"Heaven? You're all waiting to go to heaven?" Cadence asked.

"Didn't you two talk to the Chief?" Joe started. "He should have explained this a bit more for you. All those folks are from here, your town – *our town*. We lived here, we died here. We're supposed to go into the light. There is a light just like the preacher said. But, some of us are too stubborn and don't go, so we kind of missed the bus."

"So this is where you go when you 'miss the bus'?" Cadence asked.

"From what I understand, there are places like this all over the world. Egypt, Central America, England and a lot more. They are all doorways from your world to the next," Joe said. He stopped again and looked at me. "Your house is built right smack on the doorway here."

We were getting closer to the hill and could hear some conversation coming from some of the townspeople gathered there. "Look at all these people, confused and lost. I'm the only black man here. The only Asian guy is Mr. Kong; he taught math at the college and dropped dead in his driveway going to work. He came to our town from Korea during the war. I call him *King Kong* like the movie but I don't think he gets it. He's only been here for a little while now."

"And the rest?" I asked.

"They all have their own stories," he said.

"What's yours, Mr. Joe?" I asked.

He thought for a moment while his smile faded. "I'm a stubborn man, a stupid and stubborn man," he began. "I moved here from far away, too. I was born in New Orleans in 1910 and my Pop bought me my first horn when I was a kid. I loved music and played in some great bands when I was older. I was good, *real good*. Then I met Laverne and got married; once her Mamma died, we moved up here to be closer to her brother. I took a job as a janitor at the high school and gave lessons at night in my living room. I stayed at that janitor job for more than twenty years.

"We got used to the town and the town got used to us. We raised our only daughter there. One day I was home alone while Laverne was out with the ladies from her church and I died of a heart attack. I was fifty-five years old. I stood up and looked down at my body and realized what happened. There was a light shining down on my body and I could feel it pulling at me. I was real mad, *stupid mad*, and ran away and hid from the light. I was going to try and cheat; stay and try to get back into my body. I wanted to stay with my Laverne. Then 'poof,' I was here."

"Did you become a statue?" I asked. He took a moment to collect himself before going on.

"No, nothing like that. Actually, I saw one of those people just standing there, looking at the ground. I tried to talk to him, but he didn't hear me. Then I met the Fire Chief and I figured it out from there. Now I try to find the statues and shake them out of their trance; bring them here. We are waiting on this hill," Joe said, looking over the townspeople.

"What are you waiting for?" Cadence asked.

"For the last Chief, the one who will send us home," he answered, while he adjusted his hat.

****

A couple of the townspeople had noticed our arrival and a few of the women came over to greet us.

"Hello, Roosevelt; is this them?" one lady asked with a thick French accent.

"Bonjour madame, il peut attendre plus tard?" Joe said to one of them.

"When do we leave?" asked another.

"Whoa, ladies; slow down. I don't think it's time yet. Why don't you get back to what you all were doing," Joe said patiently to the ladies.

"Hey, King Kong!" Joe smiled and waved. Mr. Kong broke from his trance and gave a half-hearted wave back.

None of the men got up though a couple of them also waved. Cadence and I returned the waves; I took the opportunity to count. There were seventeen people in all sitting on the hill; there were possibly a few more spread throughout the area as "statues," unable to move. There were Joe and Tony too. Altogether it was quite a bit of people, not to mention the eight guardians.

We had met the Fire Chief; but I needed to know about the rest.

Chapter 22

"*J*oe, tell me more about the Chiefs," I said. Joe turned from the people on the hill and looked at me for a moment, sizing me up.

"There's supposed to be eight Chiefs guarding that doorway where you came in. The Chiefs were chosen over time by the folks. When the Chief died he came here to be a protector; they're supposed to keep the doorway safe. Only there ain't no eight Chiefs — they're missing one," Joe said to me.

"Where's the eighth one?" I asked.

"They might have just picked him out," he said and started walking still holding Tony's hand. We followed.

"Why all the mystery, Joe? Where are the six Chiefs I haven't met yet and why does there have to be eight? Are all of the guardians former Chiefs of the Namtuxet tribe? Why do they need to protect the doorway anyhow? Who is picking out the eighth Guardian? How are they going to get those people to wherever it is that they need to go? How long have you been here? Do you eat or sleep? Why aren't there any children?" I questioned Joe in rapid fire. I needed to know this stuff and I didn't want to overlook anything.

Joe stopped and looked me over again and said, "Maybe they chose right, after all." He started walking again and added, "I can't answer all your questions but I'll do my best. Yeah, they were all Chiefs but they can tell you about that themselves; you'll be seeing them sometime soon. Why they need eight I got no idea. Maybe they can tell you that, too. All I can tell you is that the seven Chiefs are picking *Number Eight*. As far as the doorway is concerned, I can only tell you this; they ain't protecting people from going in – they're stopping something from *coming out!*"

With Tony at his side, Joe kept walking and led us back to the doorway — back to my yard, my home. We entered the circle and found the center. The breeze had picked up a little and the grass swayed with it.

"Joe what's going to come out of the doorway? Is it bad?" Cadence asked; she looked a little sad. More likely, scared.

"Girl, you don't ever want to know such a thing," he said to her just loud enough for me to hear. "Not to worry, though. The Chiefs have been guarding the door for a long time and they know their business."

"Are we going back?" I asked Joe. He let go of Tony's hand and Tony then took our hands just as he had when we arrived.

"Tony here is the only one who can pass through; I can't, the Chiefs can't. Tony will get you home. He'll pick you up in three days and bring you back when you can meet all of the Chiefs. It was a pleasure to make your acquaintance." Joe kissed Cadence's hand and then shook mine.

"What time will he pick us up?" I asked.

"He'll just come get you, don't you worry," Joe answered with a big smile. He started to walk away from us, he was leaving the circle.

"What is that thing that we should never know? From what do the Guardians protect the doorway?" I asked Joe, as he turned his back to us.

"So many questions," he waved as he walked away. "Don't worry; you'll get your answers. I'll see you soon."

"Just tell me that one thing, Joe! What are the Guardians protecting the doorway from?" I had to yell, as he was getting too far away.

He stopped and yelled back, "Whatever it is, I call it Mr. Black!" He turned and was gone.

I looked down at Tony, who was just holding my hand, waiting. He hadn't turned around to hear Joe. "Have you seen Mr. Black, Tony?"

"No and I don't want to. The Fire Chief told me a story about him, he's a scary monster. He *eats* people," Tony said.

"Then we don't want to meet him, either," Cadence said looking at me.

"I wish he'd answered all of my questions," I said. Above us the sky grew dark and the breeze stopped and silence fell around us.

****

When I tried to look down, I felt confined. I bumped my forehead into the back of the closet door. Tony was gone, and Cadence and I were crammed up next to each other in the closet. Any other time I might have been embarrassed, being so close to her. Boy, she was pretty. But that thought lasted a split second. We could barely breath we were crammed so tight. I opened the door and the room was dark; my digital alarm clock read 8:30. If Mom wasn't already home, she would be soon Cadence and I quietly sneaked out of the room to the stairs.

I heard Mom's voice. She must have been on the phone; it sounded like she was talking to Dad. Our only chance was to head straight for the front door. Cadence and I slowly went down the stairs holding our breath. We reached the bottom and Mom was facing the other way, so we stole our way to the front door.

"...I told him that I'd be home around eight, I have no idea where he could be. No, I don't have Cadence's phone number," Mom was saying. I opened the door but it made too much noise, Mom turned. "He just walked in. Alright, I'll see you soon. Love you, too." She said into the phone then hung up.

"You were at Cadence's, weren't you? I might have known." Mom put her hands on her hips. "At least you were safe. Did you eat your supper?"

"Uh, yes; we ate over Cadence's," I lied.

"Hi Cadence, honey, how are you?" Mom smiled at Cadence.

"I'm fine, thanks Mrs. Patrick."

"Well, it's getting late and I think Cadence should go home. You two can talk tomorrow, alright?" Mom added. We both nodded and stepped out onto the porch.

We didn't say a word for a few moments. We looked around. I took in the sounds and the smells of the night air. Cadence looked to me and took my hand. She stood on her toes and kissed me on the lips; it was a brief kiss – a sweet kiss.

"Goodnight," she said and she stepped off the porch. I watched her go until I couldn't see her anymore.

****

That night was the first night in almost four years that I didn't expect a visit from Tony. I fell asleep with the lights off. Since I didn't get a chance to speak with Dad, he didn't know, and at some point in the night, he turned my light on as I slept.

****

It was Saturday morning and I didn't get out of bed until 7:30, I was awake but needed more time with my thoughts. Dad was already up excited for the big day. He said a film crew was due to arrive in an hour or so, along with Mr. Green and Mr. Topaz, and a digging crew made up of football players from the high school. He was so excited about the dig that I didn't have the heart to tell him everything I'd learned the night before. I would have to wait until it was over.

Dad and some of the younger guys from the high school did most of the digging; Mr. Green and Mr. Topaz supervised. They would get dirty when they climbed into the hole to examine the marker more closely or to point out something of interest, but Dad was a dirty mess. Several people dropped by to see and be seen, including the entire school committee and the principal of the high school. Some of the honors students came by and people driving by even stopped to see what was going on. Cadence and Manny and I just sat on the porch and watched all the hubbub, while Mom brought us sandwiches and lemonade.

The day wound down with Dad sitting on the stone marker like it was a throne, a beer in his hand. The marker was bigger than Dad had expected. It must have weighed a ton, so it had never been excavated. The men merely dug the hole around it large enough to climb in and examine five of the sides of the cube; the bottom was a loss. The video crew took plenty of film, but I figured they would have a hard time making something interesting out of hours of videotape chronicling the digging of a hole.

When everybody left, I climbed down and sat in front of Dad, and told him about Tony's latest visit. I told him about Cadence, the closet, the Fire Chief, the townspeople and Roosevelt Joseph. I didn't think it necessary to tell him about Mr. Black until I saw how he would take the entire Tony thing.

As it turned out, Dad was relieved that Tony was benign, but he said he felt awful about how lost and sad Tony was. He promised that he would try to find as much information as he could about Tony's family.

I omitted telling Dad about our expected return there. I was sure he would want to go and I don't know why, but I was afraid for him.

Chapter 23

It was late in the afternoon when Cadence and I arrived at Manny's house. Manny was outside helping his older brother clean and detail his Mustang. Manny's brother seemed so entranced in cleaning the chrome wheels that he didn't seem to even notice us, but as soon as Manny saw us, he stopped what he was doing and waved us over.

"Hi Manny," Cadence smiled and gave him a hug.

"Hi, Cadence; I'm pretty dirty," he said.

"Don't worry about it." She let go, brushing off her shirt

"Hey guys!" Manny's brother's head popped up behind the hood. "We're almost done, so Manny, you might as well go hang with your friends."

"When do I get my ride?" Manny asked, tossing a dirty rag towards his brother.

"I'll give everybody a ride in a little while. After I take a shower," he said as he gathered up his rags, waxes and tools.

"Hey, how's it going?" Manny said, sticking out his hand with no apologies for the dirt.

"Good, Manny, real good. You look like your old self," I said, shaking his hand. He did look like his old self; his eyes were clear and there were no bags. He resumed his cool demeanor and seemed genuinely happy to see me.

"I feel more like it too. I stopped taking the dope the other doctor prescribed for me and I've been seeing that shrink once a week. He's actually helping me; the nightmares come a lot less than before," he said.

"You're not mad at me then, are you?" I asked.

"Why would I be? It's not your fault. The problem is in my head." Manny started walking towards the back yard, so Cadence and I followed. "How's your spooky friend?"

"Manny, you're not going to believe this," I said.

"I believe everything so far. Can it get any weirder?"

Manny and Cadence sat on the steps of the back porch while I stood in front of them, reciting the events of the past week. I started with Tony's change, about Tony began acting out in physical ways, and I told him about my Dad finding out. I went through it all from the beginning unsure where we had left off. It had seemed so long ago the three of us were all together. I told him pretty much everything, except I neglected to recount Cadence's kiss; Manny didn't need to hear *those* details. I ended with Cadence and me winding up in my dark closet, and the archeological dig in our front yard.

Manny didn't speak through my whole dissertation; he only looked to Cadence a couple of times for affirmation of what he was hearing. She would nod and add her two cents when I took a breath. I was trying to be easy on Manny; I didn't want him to become upset over the subject matter. I also didn't want him to become upset because of Cadence, but Manny surprised me.

"Can I go with you?" he asked. I must admit that I was a bit stunned by his request.

"What?" Cadence was surprised as well.

"You want to go?" I asked incredulously.

"If it means helping you out, then yes. It's what friends do. You guys have been the best friends I've ever had," he said. He surprised me again — Manny had tons of friends.

"Manny, you really shouldn't go; we can handle this," Cadence said. I couldn't help but notice that she put her hand on his shoulders and sat a little closer to him than I expected she would.

"I can go, I *need* to go. You're my friends and you need me; I need to face my demons and overcome them. I'll do it if you want me to," he said looking back and forth between Cadence and me.

"OK, you can come," I said. "After all, we're only going to meet the Chiefs and find out how we can help getting the lost ones home. You'll like Mr. Joe, Manny; he's cool like you."

"Guys, any sign of trouble and we should get out of there as quickly as possible,"

Cadence added.

"What trouble, Cadence? We're only going to try to help them; that's all. Tony's
on our side now so I don't expect any trouble," I said.

"I don't think Joe told us everything Step. There's something more going on there. And, I don't like this Mr. Black character either; if he scares Tony, he scares me. It must take something awful to scare a dead person," she added.

"Both of you stop worrying. I'll be fine; I swear," Manny said.

I tried to read his expression; there was no sign of apprehension at all. "Manny, did you really mean it when you said that we were your best friends?" I asked.

Manny smiled. "Are you crazy? Who else would visit a kid with night terrors every day like Cadence? Who would hang around with me now that I'm seeing a shrink other than you? You both supported me when I needed it. The other guys I know want nothing to do with me now."

I was pleased that Manny thought so highly of me even though Cadence really deserved the credit for *being there* for him. I smiled back to him and patted his other shoulder as my father often did to me. Then the three of us stayed for a while, and talked about school, movie stars and television shows. For a very brief moment, we were just regular kids on a Saturday afternoon.

****

After Church, Dad asked Mr. Green and Mr. Topaz to assist him with finding the current whereabouts of the Delmarre family. Mr. Green, in turn, called Nancy Baudette and asked her to let him into the local paper's archives on Sunday. Nancy was one of the paper's editors and was a second generation member of the Historical Society, so she was happy to assist. She joined Mr. Green in leafing through files in the slim hope that there was something that would lead them to the Delmarre's. Dad said she promised to keep the research hush-hush.

Mr. Topaz drove his Ford to the police station and spoke to his former colleagues who were also very helpful. Sergeant Kane worked with former Detective Topaz for many years and would pull some strings to see what he could come up with. When asked why he needed the information, Mr. Topaz simply explained that he was trying to find his former neighbors to talk to them about the discovery of Namtuxet markers on their former property. This was pretty much the truth as far as Mr. Topaz was concerned. Sergeant Kane had heard about the markers and had no problem with helping his retired friend.

Dad hadn't told his two Historical Society friends all that had transpired at our house, just that he needed to do more research on the Namtuxet marker project. Dad explained to me that it could be some time before we found out where the Delmarre's were, if we ever found out at all. I was thankful for his help and hopeful that we would have information in time for Tony.

But, in time for what? That was the next question. I was under the impression that Tony, Joe and the rest of the townspeople were heading off to the next plane of existence where they should have gone in the first place. It was unclear what needed to be done to make that happen but it had everything to do with the Chiefs. Something was bothering me about the whole thing but I couldn't put my finger on it.

Joe said that the Chiefs were selecting the eighth guardian themselves but who could they choose? Who could they *know*?

Chapter 24

*M*onday marked three days, and that meant, sometime that day, Tony would come for me. I knew he'd wait till I got home from school. He had to, because the Portal was in my room and Cadence was supposed to be with me when Tony took us back. That and Manny wanted to go, too.

As usual, Mom used the drive time to chat about everything she could.

"Dad turned off all the lights last night and stopped keeping the lookout by sleeping on the couch," she said. "I'm glad he's back upstairs and all the lights are off, but now I think it's all the digging and writing that is getting to him."

"I'm glad he feels better," I said to her, unsure where the conversation was going or why she was talking to me like this.

"What do you think about the hole in the yard?" She asked as she turned down Elm Street.

"It's pretty cool. I sometimes think about what our property looked like hundreds of years ago, before it was occupied by European settlers." I actually *did* know what it looked like. I had seen it with my own eyes when Tony took us there.

"The hole is pretty cool?" She glanced at me.

"I meant the marker; all of the markers," I answered.

"Your Dad says that there are eight of them. Mr. Blanche told him it was OK if they dug up the last one as long as they filled in the hole when they were done. I think Mr. Blanche just wants to get on TV."

"There are only seven markers," I said mostly to myself. If they dug up Mr. Blanche's yard they wouldn't find a thing; at least that was the impression I got when the Fire Chief touched my shoulder.

"Dad and the guys from the Historical Society will find the eighth one." Mom smiled at me in the rearview. Someone honked at us from behind.

"Maybe," was all I could muster. Mom supported Dad's ideas no matter what; she really loved him and I guess that was part of the deal. Mom pulled the Volvo into the school parking lot and let me out after I leaned over so she could kiss my cheek. I was going to have to wean her off of that at some point soon. However young I was, I was in high school after all. She waved to me her whole way out of the parking lot. I looked back at her, closed the door and went into the building.

****

Manny and Cadence were waiting for me in the driveway when I came home from school. Mom said her hello's and then went into the house. Manny had his hands in his pockets, and kept raising his shoulders up and letting them fall. Cadence was twirling her hair with both hands. There was no question in my mind that they were nervous.

"Hey Manny, hi Cadence; if you still want to, come on in. Tony won't come until we're in my room," I said as I led them inside.

We had all agreed to dress in jeans and sensible shoes for the terrain. I had to change out of my school uniform, so I hid behind the door while Cadence looked out the window. I couldn't forget my camping vest. The night before, I had packed it with anything I thought we might need. I tried to think of everything. I put wooden matches and a lighter sealed in sandwich bags in my upper left pocket and two types of compasses, the kind to draw and the kind that showed due north, in my right. In the next set of pockets were pens, pencils and paper, also in plastic baggies so they wouldn't get wet. I also had a small flashlight and some extra batteries, a couple of bags of trail mix and a small tin can of lighter fluid.

The vest was hanging on the back of my desk chair; on the desk I also had set aside my Swiss Army knife, a small magnifying glass and the crucifix on a chain that I received for my first communion. I never wore it but since we were going to a sacred place with people trying to find their way to the afterlife it seemed like a good idea to have it with me.

"What do you need all this stuff for?" Manny asked.

"You never know; I just like to be as prepared as I can," I said as I put on the vest. The pockets were bulging but snapped securely. I put the items from the desk in my pants pockets. Cadence picked up the crucifix.

"I have one just like this," she said.

"Did you bring it with you?" I asked.

"No, I only have my house keys and some money in my pockets. I wasn't thinking I guess."

"Don't worry Cadence. But you might as well wear the cross. Put it on. I doubt we'll need any money, though," I said. I looked to Manny who had plopped down on the bed and asked, "Are *you* ready?"

Manny smiled and nodded, "Yeah, I'm ready. At least I think so."

I was done getting ready so I sat next to Manny on the edge of the bed. Cadence joined us and sat on my other side so that I was in the middle. We looked around and waited; I could hear the radio in the kitchen and my mother banging pots and pans. I got up and closed the door then returned to my spot on the bed.

It was a bright, sunny day and the room was filled with light. I stole glances at Cadence as she looked around the room taking inventory. Manny was doing the same; now his nerves prompted him to begin whistling. I sighed deeply; I hated waiting. I was about to get up to go get us some milk and cookies when my bedroom door handle started to turn slowly back and forth. We all stared at the handle. I looked at Cadence, whose eyes had grown as large as saucers; Manny leaned forward, finally silent and still.

My mother swung the door open with one hand; she had a dishtowel in the other.

"Pardon my wet hands; do you kids want a snack?" she asked. Manny deflated in place; Cadence had stood ready to scream.

"No thanks, Mom," I said, slightly annoyed. Manny and Cadence shook their heads simultaneously.

"Alright then; if the four of you want something just shout," she said and closed the door.

I stared at the door; did I just hear her correctly?

****

The three of us turned towards the closet. Tony was standing there in his cape and he was smiling. "You're Mom's nice," he noted.

Manny jumped back and bumped into my dresser. Cadence covered her mouth with two hands to keep from yelling; Tony had surprised the three of us.

"OK you guys, let's go," Tony said.

Chapter 25

The closet space was at a premium with the four of us in there. I went in last and closed the door, surrounding us with darkness; I felt Cadence reach for my hand. We were all connected by our hands and then I felt a breeze in my face. Gradually, the light grew and I could make out grass under my feet.

"Wow," Manny said in awe. He was right; it was awesome. The light brightened some more and I could see clouds in the sky.

"Mr. Joe should be waiting for us," Tony announced. The daylight came and Joe was standing at the edge of the circle near one of the stone markers. Once he saw us he began walking our way.

"Ladies and Gentlemen, welcome. You all are right on time," Joe said when he reached us.

"Where are we?" Manny asked Joe.

"Son, there ain't no 'where'; you are here. You are *in-between*," Joe said with a smile. He winked at Cadence then took her hand, kissed it lightly then released it. Then he came over to me and shook my hand. Leaning down to pick up Tony and put him on his shoulders, "Hey, there big fella," he said still grinning.

"I brought back three Mr. Joe. I did real good, didn't I?" Tony asked.

"You did a fine job, Tony." Joe walked over to Manny and said, "We haven't been acquainted Mr. Manny — my name's Joe." Manny took Joe's held out hand hesitantly. "It's alright son, I don't bite."

I didn't see any of the Chiefs; I thought they would come to meet us. Joe must have read my thoughts.

"Don't worry, boy. They'll be here soon," he said as he walked towards the stream in the tree line with Tony on his shoulders, gesturing for us to follow.

We stopped at the stream for a drink of its cold, clear water. Manny drank deeply and rested on a fallen tree not far from the water's edge. "No bugs," he said.

"What's that?" Joe asked.

"There are no bugs here, no bees or butterflies and definitely no mosquitoes." Manny said looking around.

"No animals either," Cadence added.

"I do not think that there are any children as well; other than Tony and the three of us, of course," I added.

"No sir; no bugs and no animals for sure; they don't belong here. As far as children go, other than Tony, none of them has ever missed the bus. I don't know why, that's just the way it is here. But I don't know about other doorway places, maybe they have children," Joe said, as he picked up a stick and examined it. Joe handed the stick up to Tony who used it to scratch his back.

We finished drinking and continued on to the hill at the edge of the meadow. There wasn't any wildlife but there certainly was plant life. The grass was rich and green; flowers of all types seemed to be in constant bloom. In a short time we reached the hill and, just as before, the townspeople were gathered about, standing or sitting, talking or lying down. I counted them; there were sixteen on the hill, when there were seventeen the other day. I went among them and started asking about it.

"Does anyone of you know if someone has gone somewhere? Has someone left this place?" I asked. Some people looked at me while others didn't or wouldn't. No one spoke up until a young woman sitting alone raised her hand. The woman was wearing a dark blue Victorian outfit.

"She's gone," she said. I stopped and knelt beside her.

"Who's gone?" I asked again.

"She, the woman sitting here." She pointed to the ground beside her.

"Did you know her?"

"Mrs. Mains I think."

"Do you know where she went?"

"Yes."

"Where?"

"The bad man came and took her away."

The conversation was difficult at best; the woman seemed like she was in some kind of a trance and had to be directed. Joe had taken Tony off of his shoulders and the pair was sitting at the bottom of the hill staring back toward the way we came. Manny and Cadence were sitting down, listening to every word of my conversation with the woman in blue. I walked over to Joe and stood before him.

"Joe, there are only sixteen townspeople on the hill, when I counted seventeen the last time I was here. I talked to one of them and she said that a woman was taken by a 'bad man.' Do you know what she's talking about?" I asked.

Joe looked up to me for a moment then back to the horizon, and sighed.

"The Chiefs will be here in a little while," he said.

"What about the missing lady?" I asked again with more urgency.

"Boy, the Chiefs will be here; talk to them." He looked at me seriously.

"Mr. Black chased her," Tony said in a little voice, "I think he *ate* her." Joe looked to him as if he was going to scold him but didn't. Tony looked very scared and very small sitting at the bottom of that hill.

"Isn't that the thing that the Chiefs are trying to keep from getting out of the portal?" I asked excitedly. Joe and Tony no longer answered. Cadence and Manny heard some of my conversation and came over to me.

"What's going on?" Cadence asked.

"I think that Mr. Black thing got out and did something with one of the townspeople," I answered. Manny looked like he was on the verge of a panic, and Cadence wasn't too far behind him.

"Oh no!" Manny shouted.

"Calm down both of you. We'll talk to the Chiefs and find out what's going on here," I said.

"I knew something wasn't right with all this! We may have to get out of here and get ourselves to safety," Cadence said.

"I'm not so sure anywhere is particularly safer than here, Cadence," I said looking to her. "The portal is in my yard. If whatever Mr. Black is can pass through it, then it can follow us."

"Here they are," Joe said and stood. He picked up Tony, put him back up on his shoulders then began to walk back towards the trees. I glanced over and saw the seven; the Fire Chief was gesturing for us to come to them. The other six were dressed similarly but not the same. From where we were I could see that some wore no shirts and others had partially shaved heads. I saw no weapons but that didn't mean that they didn't have any.

We walked back and were greeted by the Fire Chief at the edge of the trees. He bowed and the others bowed with him. He then led us back to the circle of stones where my house would be sometime in the future or on some other plane of existence. Each Chief took their position by a stone marker which I assumed meant that it was theirs. We stood together with Tony and Joe in the middle. The Fire Chief motioned to Joe.

Joe spoke, his mouth moved and it was his voice but the words seemed to come from somewhere else.

"I am here to serve you as translator and guide. I will begin with introducing the Chiefs also known as the Guardians. Then all will be revealed; you will be allowed to ask any questions that you wish; the Chiefs will answer as best as possible. We will follow with a small ceremony."

"Ceremony? What kind of ceremony?" I asked.

"Your coronation as Chief and Guardian," Joe answered.

Chapter 26

*J*oe pointed at two of the Chiefs who stood opposite each other and said, "These are the Sun Chiefs; they provide warmth and light."

The markers next to each Sun Chief had the swirl carving on it. Dad was right; it was a symbol of the sun. Joe held his arms outstretched and turned like the hands of a clock until he pointed at two other Chiefs standing across from each other.

"These are the Water Chiefs; they provide the rain that makes thing grow and quenches our thirst." The markers next to the Water Chiefs had the 'S' shaped carvings on it to signify water. Joe turned again like a clock.

"These are the Air Chiefs; they fill our lungs and fuel our flames and give flight to the winged ones." The markers next to the Air Chiefs had smaller versions of the other symbols on them. Joe turned again.

"These are our Fire Chiefs, they provide warmth when we are cold, light when it is dark and they purge us when we are foul." The marker next to the Fire Chief had the triangle on it with the point aimed at the sky. Opposite him was a stone marker that matched his own. That marker must have appeared out of thin air as I did not notice it when we arrived.

"The circle that they form represents the world of the living. On this ground is the doorway to the other worlds where the dead shall pass. The Chiefs have vowed to remain here for all time to protect those worlds from those who would cause havoc and destruction. They have been given the power by the people and only the people can take it away." Joe finished and lowered his arms. His chin rested on his chest; he was exhausted.

The Chiefs walked forward towards us in the center. Joe seemed to come back to life, and looked to us. "If you kids join hands," Joe said in his normal voice, "all three of you can hear the Chiefs."

"What's happening Joe?" I asked. Manny's shoulders were popping up and down like a pogo stick and Cadence was twirling her hair into knots. I was beginning to feel that way myself.

"Hold on a minute. The Chiefs will talk to y'all through me," Joe said. "That's why I'm here, because I can hear them and I can hear you too. I can speak with Tony and the townspeople too; the Chiefs can't," Joe said as we joined hands like a small chain.

"The Fire Chief shared his thoughts with me when he touched my shoulder last time," I said.

"Sure, the old Fire Chief sends pictures and *feelings* but it's hard to say what he's got to say that way," Joe said. "Now hold on."

The Chiefs were closing in around us, and soon formed a ring around us. They locked hands and stared straight ahead. Joe looked down at Tony and said, "Tony, my little man, you have to go out of the circle for a bit."

"I'll go sit on the new rock," Tony said, wandering over to the new stone marker my Dad had just uncovered yesterday.

Joe watched him go then turned to us, "OK, you're on."

"What do we do?" I asked.

"You can talk to them and they can talk to you," Joe answered. I could now get answers to my questions but Cadence went first.

"Why are we here?" she asked scanning the circle of Chiefs.

"They called you," Joe started. "They been here a long time and they know that their own folks are gone. They knew that they had no more chiefs; it was the end of the line. They need one more, though. They are strong, real strong, but they need one last Chief to help keep out Mr. Black."

"Who is Mr. Black?" This time it was Manny.

"He's bad, *real bad*, like the devil himself. He sometimes pushes his way through the door and finds the folks out here that miss the bus. Then he *eats* them. Since the folks are all staring at the ground like statues, they are easy pickings. That's why I try to get them back to the hill where I can keep an eye on them; I try to keep them close to the Chiefs here."

"Why me, Joe? Why do they want me to be a Chief?" I asked.

Joe walked up closer to me and smiled a little. "A Chief is three things; he is smart and that's you for sure; he is brave and that's your friend Manny here; and a Chief has love, love for life, for each other, for the world, and that's you, Cadence."

"So we're all Chiefs?" I wanted more.

"In a way, I suppose. There can only be one more Chief but your friends will teach you the rest of the things you need. Then, when you die, you will come here and help keep the good folks heading to their home and you'll help keep Mr. Black out. Do you understand?"

"I think so, but it still doesn't answer the question 'why me'?"

"Let's just say you were at the right place at the right time. See, only special people have that inner strength, the power to be a Chief and the Chiefs can tell who does. Unfortunately, none of those poor townsfolk over on the hill has what it takes."

"One day, someone actually built a house right on top of the doorway and in that house was a little boy."

"Tony," Cadence said.

"Yeah, Tony. He's got some of that strength but not enough. When he died, he wound up here, the first child to ever come. I still think the Chiefs had something to do with it," Joe said.

"The Chiefs killed Tony?" Cadence asked a bit alarmed.

"No, Tony got sick and died as he was supposed to, but most kids just go to the light when they die. Tony didn't. I think the Chiefs brought him here because Tony was strong enough to use the doorway so he could bring someone else who was strong," Joe said pointing at my chest.

"First Tony wanted to go home to find his momma but she was gone by then. He saw the baby in his room and boy, was he mad. Afterwards, he felt bad; it was only a baby after all. So he went back to see the baby but he scared the baby's momma, scared her real good. You see, Tony can project himself good, like I can. They moved away; then you came, and the Chiefs felt your power through Tony," Joe said.

"What do you mean, Tony can project himself like you?" Cadence said.

"Well Cadence, all of the folks you see here aren't really here, not physically. The way they look is the way they *think* they should look; like they did when they was alive. Tony can change himself. Most times he looks like the little boy he was when he was living but he likes those scary monsters from those old movies. That's how he tried to scare you but you don't scare so easily. Me, I like my new suit, so that's how I show you all what I look like."

"Where do the townspeople have to go?" Manny asked.

"Good question, Mr. Manny; they have to go *home*. I don't think that heaven is a bunch of dead people with wings and a harp sitting on some cloud. Life is much more than that. We are all part of *something*, something bigger then ourselves. We are like one brick in a whole building of bricks and we make up something big, something wonderful. So when we die we go to the light. We are made up of the light inside us. When we go into the light, we are like that brick going back to our spot in the wall of that building. That's the only way I can think to explain it. Hope it helps."

"How do we get them there?" I asked.

"Through the doorway; we got to convince them to go. You got to show them the way," he said, pointing to my chest again.

"I don't even know the way," I said exasperated.

"You'll figure it out," he said.

Chapter 27

$\mathcal{I}$ understood that I would spend much of eternity here but I would still have my life to live and I had two close friends to live it with.

Joe motioned to the Chiefs. "Are you ready and willing to become a Chief?" Joe asked.

"Yes," I answered.

"What are you doing?" Cadence yelled at me.

"I'm going to be a Guardian," I answered.

"You'll be here forever," she said, trying to change my mind.

"Only after I die; why else did we come back? Why are we here? We have to do something; *I* have to do something," I told her. "But I will need your support, your guidance, and your help. You heard what Joe said."

Cadence looked to Manny, who raised his shoulders again, this time as if to say he had not a clue. She raised her shoulders then too, and turned back to me, shaking her head 'yes'.

Joe turned to Cadence and Manny. "Are you both willing to teach him, to learn from him, to stay with him, and to help him get ready to be a Guardian in his dying days?"

"Yes," Cadence answered.

"Yes," Manny said.

Joe looked to me and said, "The Chiefs have prepared a marker for you. Go to it. There, you'll find a hammer and chisel. You must make your own mark on the stone. Manny and Cadence, you can help him if you want to."

We let go of each other's hands and walked through the break in the circle of Chiefs to the new marker. The stone looked fresh somehow and sat high on the surface instead of sunken or partially buried. Tony hopped down and went to Joe who had come close to watch. There were a dozen or more large logs that had their branches and bark removed so their surface was bare and smooth.

A primitive hammer and chisel made from some kind of dark, cold metal lay on the ground before it. The chisel had a pitted and crusty surface. The side of the stone facing away from the center of the circle was blank. I picked up the tools and readied to strike.

"What should I put there?" I asked my companions.

Cadence shrugged but Manny said, "Put our names on it."

"First three letters of our first names will fit," I said.

It took some doing and quite a bit of time. I did remember Joe saying that time did not have the same meaning there. I scribed our names on the stone first and began to carve. I put the chisel to the stone then struck it with the hammer, a small chunk of stone chipped away. I repeated this and quickly formed the first letter in my name. Either the stone was not as solid as we thought or the tools were better. Most likely there was some kind of magic at work engineered by the Chiefs.

I finished writing my name high on the stone so that there would be room for the next. I looked at my work. It was not pretty but it was legible. I handed the hammer and chisel to Cadence. "I'm too clumsy, I can't do this," she said.

"Sure you can," I said.

"No, can you do it for me?"

I relented and chiseled her name beneath mine. After a while I was done with that one as well. I handed the tools to Manny who had to squat to chisel his name as it was low to the ground. While he worked, I looked over to the seven Chiefs who had taken up positions by their own stones again. Joe and Tony waited patiently for us to finish. Manny was soon done with his name; it only seemed like twenty minutes had passed but it had to have been more.

"The hands of the old ones guide your hands to make quick work of the stone. You three stand here, and the Fire Chief will finish the ceremony," Joe said as he walked out of the circle with Tony in tow.

I started to empty my pockets and looked to Manny and Cadence. "Help me bury this stuff here next to my marker."

"Why you want to do that?" Manny asked.

"In case we need it later. Grab the chisel and dig," I instructed. Manny quickly dug a trench about a foot long and several inches deep. I placed the items I had in plastic in the trench and covered it up, the remaining unwrapped items stayed in my pockets. Like Manny, I wiped my hands on my pants.

The ceremony was more about the stone than about me. We stood and watched. Both Water Chiefs went to the center of the circle. There they each removed a small bladder bag of water and emptied them on the ground. They returned to their spot and the Sun Chiefs came to the center. They performed a prayer with their arms reaching for the sky. Their lips never moved; we heard the prayer in our heads. They returned to their stones and the Air Chiefs went to the center. They too made a prayer that we heard in our heads; when they were done they returned to their own markers.

Then it was our turn; the Fire Chief walked to the center of the circle as he motioned for me to join him. Once there he removed a flint rock from his bag and struck it against another rock producing sparks. He returned the items to the bag and began a prayer we all could hear.

He held out his hands, palms to the sky. As he finished his prayer, flames appeared in his hands. He held the flames up, and then clenched his fist to extinguish them. He then motioned for me to return to my stone.

As quick as that, the ceremony was over. The Chiefs remained at their stones. They turned to me and my friends as if awaiting instructions or action. I had nothing in mind and started looking for Joe and Tony; it was time for us to leave. Joe and Tony were gone and I knew somehow that they were heading for the townspeople. They were going to tell them that it was time to go and they intended to bring them back to the portal.

A glow began in the center of the portal like the flash of a camera but constant. It was small but it grew quickly. I heard the townspeople gasp far behind us. When I turned, I saw that they began to back away as if they knew what was happening. Some broke and ran for the open fields; others were frozen in place by fear.

And then it happened.

****

An incredible being between twenty and thirty feet in height comprised of total darkness appeared. It was wide and hulking yet featureless. The ground beneath it quaked with every movement and I found myself as paralyzed as some of the townspeople. The creature was as fascinating as it was frightening.

It was a living creature straight from the black and white monster movies that I watched so frequently. The roar it bellowed vibrated the very air around me and in my lungs; I felt an intense cold emanate from it. This shook me from my trance; I immediately looked for Cadence and Manny. I certainly feared for my own safety but I was more alarmed for them. They were backing away slowly out of the circle while watching the events unfold in absolute horror. I assumed this monster to be Mr. Black.

I returned my attention to the Chiefs seeking some kind of clue from them, something that would give me guidance and let me know what to do. It was a brazen appearance at the conclusion of a ceremony of the Guardian Chiefs. Did he not anticipate anyone being at the doorway at that time? The Chiefs response was to chant. I thought that they would have had more up their sleeves than chanting. Mr. Black moved about freely as if the Chiefs weren't even there. He began to walk towards the townspeople and Joe — and Tony.

The Chiefs again approached the center of the circle and I joined them, leaving Manny and Cadence to watch from my stone marker. We touched hands and that's when something amazing happened. We were one.

I could see through the same eyes that all the Chiefs saw through, we walked as one; we thought as one. It wasn't until we glanced over to Manny and Cadence that I realized that we were in one being. Now towering over Mr. Black, we grabbed him long before he got to the tree line and placed him in a bear hug, carrying him back to the portal, as he writhed in our grasp.

Once in the center of the circle again, we forced Mr. Black to the ground. We were on top of him and pressing him *into* the ground. He began to submerge as if the ground was swallowing him; I knew that he was going back through the portal to his own place and time. Mr. Black was not too happy about it and let out a scream that we felt through every molecule of our body. I even saw the trees shiver. But we were unmoved and continued to force him down.

He lashed out and broke from our grip, lunging at Manny and Cadence. They broke into a run but he grabbed Manny by the shirt collar and lifted him close to his face. Manny dangled there helpless. Mr. Black opened his gaping yaw but we regained our hold in time to stop his arm from rising. Again we forced him into the ground, back through the portal.

But, he would not release Manny, however hard Manny struggled against his grip. I knew that the Chiefs did not want Manny to perish but would not stop trying to remove Mr. Black. They were unrelenting, forcing him into the ground. I knew if I did nothing, Manny would go with him. I thought of Cadence and the crucifix I'd given her. It could be a strong talisman against Mr. Black, hopefully strong enough to drive him to release Manny.

We projected our thoughts to Cadence; she bravely ran close to the giants struggling before her. Removing the crucifix from her neck, she reached towards Manny, but the massive flailing arms of Mr. Black kept her at bay. Mr. Black was almost gone from sight, his arm and head the only things left visible above ground. Manny fought desperately against the grip of the massive hand.

Then Mr. Black was gone. The Chiefs and I parted and we were back to our own identities once more. I was deposited near my stone so I ran to the center of the circle looking for the portal, hoping it was there. My hand passed into something and disappeared into the ground to my elbow. I had found the doorway; I yelled for Manny.

Then something gripped my hand, I was sure it was Mr. Black. Whatever it was, it was heavy. I pulled and struggled then Cadence ran over to me to help. She grabbed me around the chest from behind and pulled. My hand appeared above the ground and it was wrapped around another hand; Manny's. I couldn't budge it any further and I thought that I would lose my grip.

Another hand grabbed Manny by the wrist and pulled, it was the Fire Chief. Manny flipped up and out, above ground, and we all fell back with the release. Manny was back, apparently undamaged. He sat on the ground sucking in air, exhausted. He smiled at me and reached under his collar; he pulled out his own crucifix. He had also gotten the message.

We had seen Mr. Black and we had defeated him, at least for the time being. With Manny and Cadence safe, it was time to go home.

That was when the Chiefs told us that we had one more job to do.

Chapter 28

With my induction as a Guardian Chief, the circle was now complete, and the Chiefs were eager to send the townspeople on their way to safer havens as quickly as they could, before Mr. Black regained strength and returned. They sent Joe and Tony to retrieve as many of them as they could to bring them back to the circle. When they said that Mr. Black ate people whole, I was relieved that Manny hadn't heard them, but I still felt badly for putting Manny in such danger.

Manny was the one person to return from a glimpse of the dark realm in that netherworld Mr. Black called home.

"Manny, what did you see? What was it like where Mr. Black comes from?" Cadence had beaten me to the punch. He looked at her with large eyes.

"It's very dark and cold; it feels like *death*," he said as he rubbed his goose bump-covered arms. He seemed to have had recovered but I was apprehensive that he would suffer an emotional setback. Still, he was being brave for us. "He tried to put something down my throat; something to choke me. Thank God you pulled me out."

Cadence gently rubbed his back, I tried not to notice.

The Chiefs were expecting me to come up with a way to get them home, but according to Joe they had to go of their own volition. I supposed that it was a matter of salesmanship and for that, I was not adequately equipped. They needed to *want* to go home; all of them.

But watching Cadence rubbing Manny's back gave me an idea. It was incomplete and far from my best idea, but it would be a good place to start. Joe had mentioned that each of us had our own strengths: intelligence, bravery and love. Cadence had "love for life, love for each other and love for the world," according to Joe and the Chiefs. Love would have to show them the way. Cadence would need to inspire them.

"Cadence, I think you can get the people to listen to us. You can make them want to go home," I said.

"How can I do that?" She looked concerned.

"Love, somehow love has to find a way."

"Love? What the heck are you talking about?" She went from concerned to confused.

Joe, Tony and a dozen of the townspeople arrived at the edge of the circle closest to the stream. Joe had them spread out on the boundary so that they all had a clear view of us. I sensed the Chiefs' concern for those who had chosen to remain on the hill. But, although this was their choice and they were responsible for it, the Chiefs knew I would return soon to help change their minds.

I moved to the center of the circle and beckoned the ones who came to venture closer.

"Please join me in the center of the circle. Joe, and Tony, you too," I said in a loud, clear voice. Joe and Tony walked in, joining Manny, Cadence and me.

"If Mr. Black comes back, you'll protect me, won't you Step?" Tony said to me.

"Yes, of course I will." I answered smiling down at him. I'd grown to feel protective of Tony, as if he was a little brother. But Tony didn't smile back; he was too scared. Joe wasn't smiling either, but he was there. I looked to the townspeople and beckoned again.

"Come on, we don't have all day. Don't you want to go home?" I asked.

"I don't know where 'home' is, kid," a man in a worn suit and felt hat said to me. I reached over to Cadence and grabbed her hand. She took Manny's hand.

"Do you know where you are now?" I asked him.

"Not really," he answered.

"Are you aware that you're dead?" I asked, scanning the faces before me.

"Yeah, I kinda got that idea a while back. Ain't this heaven?" he asked, looking straight into my eyes.

"No, this is not heaven. You're stuck somewhere in between," I said.

"Like Purgatory?" he parried, the other townsfolk began to crowd us.

"Sort of, I guess. But it's time to move on now, you need to go home," I said to the group.

"How do we do that?" he asked, his face a mix of confusion, apprehension and even anger.

"Your families and friends will be waiting for you," Cadence added, looking at me then back at them.

"Will my husband be there?" one of the younger looking ladies asked.

"I truly believe so," Cadence answered.

"But you're not sure?" the younger lady asked her.

Cadence didn't know for sure, but she said, "I know he will. Somehow I just know."

Then it came to me. "Miss, just give me your hand," I said, holding out my hand. She hesitated, looking to my face then my hand then back to my face. "Take my hand, please," I said in as soft a voice as I could. She finally took my hand gently and I wrapped mine around hers; we looked like we were shaking hands.

I could see her with her husband. They were laughing; they were in love. I relived her memories with her and, intertwined with her memories, were memories of mine. It was as if two movies were playing at the same time on one screen. I felt her horror and anguish when she found out her husband was killed in action during the war. I felt her disbelief at her own death from pneumonia only a few months later. She had stood over her own body for some time before she realized that she was here, wherever here was.

Then we shared my feelings for Cadence; my love felt much like her own for her husband. When I let go of her hand I realized that I was still holding Cadence's with my other. Cadence looked at me; I could see a flood of emotion on her face. She kissed my cheek; I breathed in when she was close.

I felt Manny's hand on my shoulder; his apprehension had waned. He even had a slight smile on his face, as if he understood some inside information which, in fact, was exactly the case. I had forgotten my ability to broadcast images and feelings just as the other Chiefs could. I had shared everything with everyone around me. They felt it to a lesser degree than those of us holding hands, but they got the message just the same.

I could sense that all of the townspeople had lost some, if not most, of their fear of the unknown. They trusted us; they trusted me. Most of all, they had been ready to move on the whole time but were afraid of where they would go. With the open channel I shared with the Chiefs, they began to realize they could go to the light where they belonged. The young lady walked to the center of the circle, and kissed my cheek on her way by.

I made sure that I shook the hand of everyone entering the circle, all the while holding Cadence's hand for strength. This momentary touch served as both a customary gesture and provided a brief contact that enforced the emotions we all had just shared. Soon, they were all in the center of the circle. The Chiefs remained at their markers for this entire time. Only the Fire Chief smiled.

I went to Joe and Tony and asked, "How do I start the doorway? How do I get it to open?"

"You need to do that, too," Joe said to me. "Tony and I are going home now. You and Cadence and Manny are on your own. You are a Chief, little man. You are a fine Chief, too."

"But I thought Tony was the only one who could pass through the door?" I asked, somewhat alarmed at the news.

"No, he ain't the only one. You, Cadence and Manny came through that same doorway just like Tony. You got all the tools you need right here," Joe said pointing to my chest.

"Besides, I can't let Tony go alone. I got to keep him company."

"What about the rest of the townspeople back on the hill; aren't they going?" I asked.

"You have to clean up that mess now Chief!" Joe smiled. "Now say goodbye to Tony."

I bent over and looked down at the little boy in the black cape. Not long ago he was a scary monster under my bed; now he looked like a lost little boy who wanted to go home. I knelt down and roughed up his hair. Cadence knelt beside me.

"Thanks for helping us, Tony. We couldn't have done it without you."

"Yeah, I like you, too. You can have my room, I won't need it anymore," he said to me.

"My Dad's looking for your folks; he'll find them for you." I wasn't sure what else to say.

"I know... tell them that I love them and I miss them. Tell them I'm OK; tell them that I have my friend Joe to play with," he said and he wrapped his arms around my neck. I felt his breath warm on my cheek; it smelled sweet.

"Goodbye Tony," Cadence said. A tear dripped from one of her eyes. Tony went over and hugged her too.

"Bye Cadence," he said to her.

"Bye Tony," Manny said holding his hand out palm up. Tony slapped the hand and looked up to him.

"Bye Manny." He smiled.

I stood and shook Joe's hand. He smiled widely at me. He moved to Manny to shake his hand. He reached over to Cadence and kissed her cheek, and he whispered to her, "Love always finds the way." Then he took Tony's hand and joined the group in the center. They nervously shuffled, moving side to side as if they had to go to the bathroom. The air was electric with emotion.

The Chiefs again approached the center and joined hands when they were close enough. This time, Cadence and Manny and I joined the ring too. The Chiefs began chanting in a low tone and I felt a charge pass through me. Still, nothing happened.

"You gotta push it, from inside," Tony yelled over to me, "kind of like holding your breath and then pushing it out again."

I tightened my stomach muscles, the charge focused there as if directed. I closed my eyes and created an image in my mind of the doorway opening; I could see it in my mind's eye. I saw a bright light and then I heard a 'pop' like a fuse had blown. I opened my eyes.

They were gone.

Chapter 29

*W*e had to get home. My mother was sure to check on us sooner or later. Joe had told us earlier that time had no meaning there and I hoped it was true. Manny, Cadence and I moved to the center of the circle and joined hands once again. The Chiefs bowed to us; the Fire Chief even waved; he must have seen one of us doing that.

The battle with Mr. Black had taken its toll on Manny, who was rubbing his stomach as if he was nauseous. Cadence looked to me as if to say, "We should hurry."

The Chiefs closed their eyes and began their chant. I looked around at the familiar yet dissimilar landscape that was my home and would be for eternity. I knew I would be back again before long; some townsfolk who needed to be convinced to go home remained on the hill.

The world faded to black and I bumped my head on the closet door. We were home. I opened the closet door. My bedroom was still bathed in light. I could hear the news on the radio in the kitchen and my mother opening draws and banging pots.

I looked at Cadence and Manny. All of us had grass stains and dirt on our clothes and our hands, and from the tracks on the floor, on the soles of our shoes as well. I noticed that Manny's skin had taken on a green sheen just as he said, "I have a stomach ache. I need to go home and lie down."

"You've had quite a day, Manny. Should we walk you home?" I said.

"Yeah, you look like you're going to get sick any minute," Cadence added.

Manny was trying to be stoic. He patted my shoulder and said, "It's not that bad; I must have pulled something when I was fighting that...thing. I'll be alright; I just need to take a nap." Then he took a breath and whispered to me, "You really love her that much, huh?"

I didn't know what to say and even felt a little embarrassed. After all, she was supposed to be his girlfriend.

"That's OK; I think it's great," Manny said, as he looked to Cadence. "Take good care of her now; she's my friend too." Cadence smiled and hugged Manny, who hugged her back as he turned to leave.

"I'll see you tomorrow, Manny," I said.

He opened the door, walked to the stairs, but didn't respond. I heard my Mom say, "Goodbye, Manny!" as he let himself out the front door.

"You really love me that much?" Cadence asked, looking into my eyes. She was close to me again. I tried not to get too excited.

"Yes," I said, which was all I needed to say because she threw her arms around me and kissed me on the lips. I kissed her back clumsily kissing part of her cheek when I closed my eyes, but she didn't seem to mind.

"Ahem," Mom said from the doorway. We jumped away from each other.

"Hi Mom."

"Is Cadence staying for dinner?" Mom asked.

Cadence looked to her sheepishly and shook her head 'no'.

"OK, you two behave; and leave this door open," she said as she smiled and turned. We stood and waited for her to disappear down the stairs, and when I heard her clanging pots again in the kitchen, I turned back to Cadence and asked, "Will I see you tomorrow?"

"Of course," she said. "I'd better go now though."

I stayed upstairs looking out my bedroom window, as I watched her go down the stairs. I heard Mom say, "Goodbye, Cadence," as the front door opened and closed. I went to the window and watched Cadence wave back to my Mom as thoughts of her raced through my head. I pictured her just moments ago, and thought of the Chiefs, the circle of markers and Mr. Black. So much had happened in such a short period of time. As Cadence rounded the corner and was out of sight, I turned from the window and saw something on the bed — a small white bundle. I went to it and picked it up. It was Tony's white mask from the *Phantom of the Opera*. I had left it there when I removed it to wipe away his tears. I sat on my bed and held it; at one time that same mask was the object of fear and horror. I stood and went to my sock drawer; I tucked the mask inside for safe keeping. Now it was a keepsake.

****

When Dad got home, I told him I had a lot to tell him. After dinner my father retired to his easy chair as he always did. But, instead of reading the paper, he called me over.

I told him about Joe and the Chiefs, Tony and the townspeople, the power of being a Chief. I recounted the whole story except for the part about Mr. Black. For some reason I felt it best not to tell him. He listened to every word without interruption. When I was done I could see disbelief in his face even though he had seen Tony with his own eyes.

"That's a pretty amazing story," he said to me with a wry smile. "Well, I'm proud of you. Now I can tell the other members of the Historical Society that my son is a Chief."

"OK, Dad; you don't have to believe me about that if you don't want to."

"No son, I do believe you, really," he said, but his eyes told a different story.

He reached into his pocket and pulled out a folded piece of paper. "Here, you wanted this."

"What is it?"

"It's the current address of the Delmarre Family. Mr. Green and Mr. Topaz got the information for you."

"I can't imagine those two working together on anything," I said.

"Actually, they are the best of friends. Mr. Green went to the real estate agent who sold the house. The Delmarres had requested some assistance in finding a house in Cambridge. Mr. Topaz found out that Mr. Delmarre got a job working for the city and one thing led to another. So now you have the address. What will you do with it?"

I thought for a moment; I had originally planned on giving it to Tony but he was in the light where he belonged.

"I might write a letter to them," I said thoughtfully.

"Well, let me look at it before you mail it. I don't want you to go and upset them; they've been through a lot," Dad advised.

"Yes, Dad; we've all been through a lot," I said.

****

On Tuesday, I kept my appointment with Dr. Erkahn and it went better than I thought it would. I told him about Manny and Cadence and he told me he was pleased that I was developing feelings towards others and was able to process the emotions. I didn't tell him about the Tony saga nor did I go into detail about my relationship with Cadence. When I left, I felt better having talked with him. I even looked forward to my next visit.

Manny had taken ill. He had some kind of digestive issue. Cadence and I were worried that maybe he had sustained internal injuries during his struggle with Mr. Black. By Wednesday, Cadence learned from his mother that his internals were fine and that they thought it was some kind of infection. He was put on antibiotics but missed a whole week of school. He was treading dangerously; if he missed too much more of school he could be forced to stay back. Cadence and I had visited him during the week and he seemed to be getting stronger; he expected to be back at school the following Monday. We were relieved.

On Saturday our house, again, was the destination for the Historical Society members and a film crew. They were digging up the stone just over the boundary in the Blanche's yard — my stone. I knew what they would find there and was curious what their take on it would be. The dig was a little more difficult than the one in the front yard. Mom had ordered Dad to fill in the other hole days earlier and he reluctantly complied.

A maple tree had grown about 10 feet away and the lattice work of its root system was hampering the dig. Finally, late in the afternoon, the hole was dug wide enough and deep enough that the markings could be seen. From a distance, Cadence and I watched the bustle of activity and conversation as they worked. But as soon as the stone was uncovered, everyone stopped talking, and started looking our way. Dad waved us over.

"Can you explain this, young man?" Mr. Green said sternly to me. He pointed at the large stone, the top of which was two feet below ground before the dig. We were facing our house with the Blanche's house behind us and I was close enough to the edge of the hole. I could see the stone and carved on it was part of our three names.

The men were a mix of confusion and anger and it was reflected in their voices. Why would you vandalize a stone with historical significance?" Mr. Green added.

"Alvin, how could he have done this? You saw how difficult the dig was; how the roots of the trees had grown over the stone." Dad was defending me.

"What did he do, go back in time?" Mr. Topaz asked.

"Did you find anything else?" I asked them. They stopped arguing among themselves.

"What else should be there?" Dad asked. I was thinking of the plastic wrapped supplies we had placed in the shallow trench next to the marker. The stone in the hole was down to the base so they would have dug up anything that had been there. It was possible that those items didn't survive through time and space. It was possible that they were on a different plane of reality. I wasn't sure.

"Nothing, I guess," I said and they all started arguing again. Mr. Topaz was trying to get my attention. I ignored them and took Cadence by the hand. We went into my house where Mom had some Oreos and milk waiting for us.

Book 2 - Mr. Black

Chapter 30

*M*anny had begun to come to my house regularly; his fears apparently had abated. I was genuinely happy to see him doing so well and pleased that he supported the budding romance I had with Cadence. I began to find myself confiding in Manny, even asking his advice on the whole girlfriend thing.

Cadence was now the center of my attention. She was my muse and confidant. We spent most every day together. My mother and father enjoyed her as well as Manny's company and were happy that I was developing deep relationships with my peers. For the few weeks that followed, our adventure into the other side my life headed into the uncharted territory of happiness.

But we still had work to do. We had to return to find the remaining townsfolk. Manny, of all people, urged me to return, but I found myself hesitant. Things were going so splendidly. For once I was a regular kid doing kid things with kid friends. I didn't want to do something that would change that.

I believed, because time had no meaning there, it would be possible to return to the moment after our last departure. For the meantime, I focused on the book that my father was writing with the Historical Society about the history of the town. He had made the markers a feature. He knew that I had inside information and wanted to include it in his work.

Mr. Topaz and Mr. Green would not stop asking me about the last marker and how our names happened to be found there. They were convinced that there was something more to the story. They were right, of course; but it would be a while before they would find out the ending—because I still had to find it out for myself.

Manny spent time with me in my room, always first checking under the bed or in the closet. We would then hang out like we did when our friendship was new; we talked of school and girls. The conversation would inevitably return to our friend Tony but mostly to Mr. Black. Why Manny's fear had changed into fascination I only began to understand after that May day in the woods.

****

On a fine day in late May, Manny, Cadence and I were behind my house on the trail near the stream. It was a tight fit, but the three of us were sitting on the marker as so many people had done over the centuries. Cadence leant against me, holding my hand; Manny had his back to us. The past few days he'd been acting a bit manic. I thought maybe his medication had changed.

"You have a birthday coming up," Cadence said to me.

"Yeah, it's on Memorial Day this year; the thirtieth. We have the day off from school. Do you guys want to do something?"

"That's next Monday! We have to spend it together, just the three of us. I'll bring a cake," Cadence said.

"We should go back to the townspeople on the hill," Manny said.

He had been hinting at this with increasing regularity. I supposed it was time that I relented.

"OK, Manny. Let's do it," I said.

"Good. I'll make preparations," Manny said in a dull tone.

"What preparations do you need to make?" Cadence asked, beating me to the punch.

"Uh, oh, I'll bring some supplies or something. Let me know what we'll need," Manny's voice returned to normal.

"Any thoughts Cadence?"

"I guess; we *should* do something for those poor people. I just hope we don't run into Mr. Black again," she said.

"I don't think we need to worry about that," Manny said.

I began to think that maybe I'd been wrong about Manny. This change in him didn't seem as simple as a result of medication. There was something more disconcerting there, but I couldn't tell what it was.

"What makes you so sure?" Cadence asked.

"Oh I don't know. I'm just trying to be brave," he said. He pushed her shoulder playfully and she smiled.

"I'm heading home. You guys want a snack?"

"Sure!" Manny said as he stood up, facing me, his smile a little too wide. What was wrong with him? Something was up.

I glanced at him, wondering and, for a split second, I thought his eyes were black. They looked like they had no whites and no brown cornea. Just all black. He looked away and I stood and went up to him. He was looking back at me with normal eyes.

"Problem Chief?" he asked. He had taken a defensive posture and clenched his fists. He looked ready to fight and happy at the thought of it. Cadence, just getting up, seemed to have missed the entire exchange.

"No," I said.

"Let's go then," he said, smiling widely.

He led the way, and we followed. The stream was as full as it could be with rushing water. It was still only about six feet wide and we crossed on some large field stones we had found and placed strategically in the water. Dad said he wanted to build a small bridge because we were out there so much.

Dad and the men from the dig had removed small trees and cleared brush on the path that led from the marker directly to our backyard. The path was now completely unobstructed and so we arrived back at my house quickly.

Manny climbed the stairs to the back porch and held open the door to the kitchen for Cadence, who was directly behind him. My mother greeted us with a plateful of Oreos; three glasses of milk were on the table. We had barely thanked her and sat down when Manny stuffed a whole cookie in his mouth, chewing it violently. Again, Cadence didn't seem to notice but I was watching him closely. We ate in silence. By the time we were finished, Manny seemed himself again. And for the moment, at least, I was relieved.

Chapter 31

*A*fter Manny left, I pulled Cadence aside, out of hearing range of my mother.

"Have you noticed anything different about Manny lately?"

"Only that he's more like he used to be; I think the psychologist is helping. Why, what do you think?" Cadence asked.

"I'm not sure," I said, which wasn't a complete lie, "but something is different about him. Keep an eye on him and let me know if you see anything out of the ordinary."

Cadence seemed to think for a moment, processing my request and possibly figuring out my angle; after all, she was rather intelligent. The moment passed, however, and she kissed my cheek. "I'll let you know." She smiled brightly, went to the front door, waved and let herself out.

I returned to my room and thought about Manny. His eyes had been black. I was sure of it. I saw them as plain as day. The black went away, but I couldn't tell whether he made that happen or it happened without his knowledge. Did this have something to do with Mr. Black? I had so many questions and no one to answer them.

Maybe Manny could answer them. I decided to have a private conversation with him before we returned to the Chiefs. If Mr. Black had done something to Manny, I worried how the results would manifest themselves in our world, and went we returned back there too. Manny was only in the netherworld briefly, but, as Joe said, time has no meaning there. Those seconds he was trapped could have been minutes or even hours. We had no way of knowing.

I was reasonably sure that no earthly illness could have caused Manny's eyes to go completely black for one moment only to return to normal the next. As our time to return drew near, my concern grew. Alongside it came an unfamiliar feeling in my stomach, a churning and turning, a worry and dread mixed together. I surmised this was what the rest of the world called "gut instinct."

****

"Step, wake up!" A little voice seemed to e calling me from somewhere nearby. "Step, please wake up!" Next, a little hand was pushing against me. I opened my eyes; it was still dark outside and in the room.

"Step," The little voice said more clearly. I turned to see Tony standing beside the bed. I was more than surprised.

"Tony? What are you doing here? I thought that you went with Mr. Joe," I said sitting up.

"Mr. Joe sent me here to warn you," Tony said.

"Warn me about what?"

"Mr. Black is coming for you, all of you. I'm so scared, Step, and I don't think that I can help you this time," Tony said on the verge of tears. I thought for a moment, allowing myself some time to process the information.

"How is Mr. Black coming for us? I thought that he was trapped on the other side."

"He is using somebody to help him," Tony said in a little more than a whisper. I became alarmed. Who would help Mr. Black invade the physical world?

"Who is helping him, Tony?"

Tony climbed onto the bed; he arranged the blankets so that he had a level place to sit and said, "I'm not sure, Step, somebody that doesn't know that they are being used. Mr. Black is tricky like that."

"What should I do?" I asked Tony hoping he came with some guidance along with the warning.

"I don't know but Mr. Joe says that you'll find the helper. He says that you're good at that stuff," Tony said.

"I don't even know where to begin."

"You'll know. I have to go now, Step. I'll try to come back and help you if I can. Mr. Joe told me to tell you guys that he says 'Hey'."

"Can you find your way back to Mr. Joe?"

"Yeah, it's easy."

"Alright then, go back to him and be safe."

"I hope that you guys can stay safe, too. G'bye Step," Tony said and gave a little wave. He began to fade into thin air like a wisp of smoke.

"Goodbye, Tony," I said. It took a while to go back to sleep.

****

After school, the next day, Mom picked me up and drove me home as usual. I was glad the week was over. I was still thinking about how to best approach Manny when we turned into our driveway and saw him sitting alone on our front steps.

"Hello Manny," Mom said as she climbed the stairs and let herself into the house.

"Hello," Manny responded. He waited until she was inside and the doors were closed then said, "Hey, how are you?"

"Fine, and you?" Even I noticed that Manny wasn't usually this stiff.

"I...I'm not so sure." He looked worried.

"What's the matter, Manny?"

"I don't feel right, like I'm not myself," he said and stood. He stuck his hands in his jean pockets and looked down at his feet.

"In what way? Can you explain it?" I asked.

Manny kept looking down at his shoes then up around us, and then back at his shoes again. I gave him time to answer, but I wondered how long it would take.

"Sometimes I don't feel like I'm here," he finally said.

"Where do you feel like you are?" I would have to pull it out of him.

"No, no. What I mean is that sometimes it's morning and I'm getting ready for school then the next thing I know it's lunchtime and I don't remember anything that happened in between." He looked up at me and he looked terrified.

This did not sound good. "How often does that happen?"

"Almost every day."

"It sounds to me as if you're experiencing blackouts. I read about them in the waiting room at my doctors. How long do they last?"

"It's not like I'm a drunk or something," Manny said as if I thought he should be ashamed. "Sometimes it's only for a few minutes; sometimes it's for a few hours."

"Have you told your psychologist about this?" I asked.

"Not yet, my next appointment is on Tuesday. This just started happening a couple of days ago."

"How do you know that you're not imagining it?" I asked.

"Because it seems like I'm doing something one minute then all of a sudden I'm somewhere else the next. It's like a bad editing job on a movie. Step, I'm more scared now than I was with the night terrors." He looked up at me, searching, as if I was the only one who could explain.

"Are you still getting those?"

"No, thank God. Those haven't come back."

"Have you mentioned this to Cadence?"

"No, nobody but you."

I could tell that something had been wrong with Manny. Now Manny knew it too. His fear told me that he had no control over it, which alarmed me more than a little.

"Alright. It's Friday, so you won't be able to get an appointment to see your psychologist until Monday. You should stay around people as much as you can. Tell your brother; he seems sympathetic and capable of watching out for you when you're home. The rest of the time you should stick with Cadence and me; we'll watch over you together."

Manny managed to smile a little at that and seemed relieved.

"I'm lucky to have you and Cadence as friends," he said.

"That's what we're here for," I said, patting his shoulder twice.

We sat on the porch for a while without talking. Our silence wasn't broken until sometime later when my mother came to the door and said, "Anyone want cookies?" We followed her inside.

****

Manny promised to talk to his older brother and went home. Mom had a cookbook open and was banging pots and pans again; I knew she was experimenting. It wasn't often she would try something out of the ordinary and sometimes it was a pleasant surprise; sometimes it wasn't.

It was my birthday this Sunday. I didn't tell Manny because he had his own problems. I didn't want him to feel obliged to me. Anyway, we were supposed to visit my Grandma again on Sunday. My birthday was less on my mind than my plans to borrow the video camera again. I wanted to bring it with us when we returned to the Chiefs so we could document our excursion there. It would prove to Dad that what I had told him was indeed fact. I wasn't sure why adults were so skeptical; Dad had seen Tony with his own eyes, yet he doubted my story about the Chiefs.

I called Grandma ahead of time to ask if I could use the camera again. She said, of course, and that she would love to see the footage when I was done. I wasn't so sure she would. I thought again of Manny and those black eyes. He was the one who wanted to return so badly but would he be up for the trip when the time came?

Chapter 32

*O*n Saturday, Manny, Cadence and I spent the day at our new favorite spot on the trail behind my house. He seemed to be holding himself together and assured me he would be able to make the trip with us to see the Chiefs. I had watched for the return of the blackness in his eyes but hadn't seen it since the first time. I began to relax a little about the whole thing. By the time they went home, we had thrown a hundred pebbles in the rushing water of the stream.

We celebrated my birthday with cake and ice cream at Grandma's house on Sunday. My parents had given me a video camera of my own so I no longer needed to borrow my grandmother's. I had no real hobbies and my parents thought that my interest in video making might become one. They suggested that I consider joining the Audio/Video club in the fall and Dad even joked that I could be the next Steven Spielberg.

The camera was similar to Grandma's LXI from Sears but the new one was a Sony. It sat on the user's shoulders and had a handle with a strap; the record button was trigger activated. It took full size VHS tapes that could go directly into the VCR from the camera; they even included the tripod. I couldn't have imagined a better present.

The next day was Monday - Memorial Day. It was a warm and sunny kickoff to the summer season. Traditionally my folks would go to a cookout at one of the neighbors houses for a couple of hours then return when things got too rowdy. Neither were big drinkers. After a couple of beers, my Dad was usually done for the night.

When I was too young to be left alone, I had to go with them but for the past couple of years I had been able to stay home. I planned on staying home again and having Cadence and Manny over to join me. Their parents were attending the party too, so when I asked if they could come, their parents said yes right away. After all, the party was at the Blanches next door.

Around noon, Cadence arrived with a cake as she had promised, and Manny came in a few minutes later. Mom helped us cut the cake, and Dad came down. They all sang "Happy Birthday" to me; Manny was full of energy and he had a huge silly grin on his face. He was fun, but I wondered if he was in the middle of a blackout.

We passed the time on the porch, waiting for Mom and Dad to go next door to the party. Manny was full of questions.

"How many townspeople do you think are still there?" he asked.

"Five, maybe more," I said. "We'll have to look for the ones who Joe called 'statues' and hopefully we can coax them along.

"It always seems like daytime there. Do you think it ever gets dark?" Manny asked.

"I don't know. We could ask the Chiefs when we get there," I said.

"Are either of you scared of Mr. Black?" This time he appeared to be addressing Cadence; she looked like she was already tired of his questions.

"No," I answered.

"Yes," Cadence said. "Manny, can you please knock it off?"

"Sorry Cadence, I'm just excited." He looked to me, "Let's go."

Manny's hands balled into fists again. I wondered if he even knew he was doing that.

"We have to wait a few more minutes until my mother and father leave. Hold your horses."

He stood up and began to pace back and forth, until Mom and Dad appeared at the door; Dad had on some chino shorts and Mom was wearing a summer dress. Both wore sandals and this time, at least, Dad wasn't wearing socks with them.

"We're heading next door, guys," Dad announced as he walked past us.

"Behave yourselves," Mom said and gave my cheek a kiss. "If you get hungry stop by; Mr. Blanche said he has enough for everyone and then some."

"Yes, Mom," I answered, but they were already walking across the front lawn towards the Blanches'.

Manny let himself into my house so Cadence and I followed. He bounded up the stairs directly to my room and we followed him up. Sunlight bathed the room in light.

"Are you feeling alright?" Cadence asked.

"Sure," Manny said.

"Did you have a lot of sugar today or something?" she asked.

"Actually, yeah; frosted flakes and a donut and chocolate milk." He smiled.

Cadence seemed satisfied with the answer. I did not let on that I wasn't. I grabbed my new video camera from my bureau and I attached the battery pack on the back of the camera; it was ready and loaded with a new tape.

"Manny, did you bring anything?" I asked.

"Uh, no; was I supposed to?" He looked puzzled.

"Yes. The other day you said you needed to make preparations. You were going to bring stuff," I said.

"Oh, well you never said what I should bring." He smiled again. "Are you guys ready?"

"I'm never ready for this," Cadence answered.

"Me either," I said and I took her hand.

"Aw, look at the lovebirds," Manny cracked. Cadence gave him a look then offered her hand and he took it. We went into the closet. Manny closed the door and, the bright summer day was gone.

Manny and Cadence remained quiet while I concentrated. I wasn't sure if they were concentrating as well but I assumed that they were. I controlled my breathing and focused the images in my mind. There was a gentle breeze and the light began to penetrate the darkness. Our eyes adjusted as the light grew brighter, and then, we were there.

We found out that it wasn't always sunny in the land of the Chiefs. The day was overcast; even a little cold. It may have been 60 degrees but we were dressed in shorts and t-shirts for the summerlike day we just left behind. I decided that I would keep the camera running the whole time and began filming. I carried it by the handle on top and held it as steady as I could; it would film from my hip area and give me more freedom. I would not have to pay attention to the camera as much.

No one was there to greet us so we made our way to the stream and onto the fields beyond. I held Cadence's hand and Manny followed behind us. Two men in early twentieth-century suits were sitting on the hill; no one else was in sight. I approached and greeted them.

"Hello gentlemen. Weren't there five of you on the hill the last time I was here?"

They looked to each other, then to me. The one in the blue suit and straw hat stood up. His partner, in a brown suit and a brown felt fedora hat, stayed seated.

"Where have you been? We've been waiting here all day."

"You should have gone with the others the last time we were here," I said.

"What others? We're the only ones here," the standing man said.

"Weren't you here during our last visit?" I asked.

"Kid, I ain't never seen you before. We were out in the woods over there then came to this here hill; now you're here and that's all I know," he said, somewhat aggressively.

"Weren't there some other people waiting on this hill?" I was a bit confused.

"No kid, don't you listen? Nobody was here – no one." He folded his arms. If they had just gotten there, where were the townspeople who refused to go the last time?

"How did you guys get here?" I asked. Now it was his turn to look confused; he unfolded his arms and put his hands in his pants pockets.

"I'm not really sure; we both work in a bank," he said, pointing to his companion, "and last thing I remember is some goons came in with guns. It was a stick-up and we gave them all our money but the goons thought we were hiding more. Last thing I remember is their guns went off..." He trailed off then looked at his companion who stood up at that point.

"Are we, you know..." the man in the brown suit started.

"Dead. Yes, you are both dead," I answered.

"Then where are we?" Brown suit asked.

"I don't know what you'd call it, but let's just say that we have to get you home," I answered.

"What's that thing?" Blue suit said pointing to the video camera.

"Movie camera," I answered. I turned around to look back at the way we came and noticed that Manny was gone. I was still holding onto Cadence but Manny was nowhere to be seen. "Where's Manny?" I asked already knowing that no one could answer.

"Do you suppose that he stayed in the woods by the stream?" Cadence guessed.

That was a possibility; my attention had been on the two men sitting on the hill.

"I don't really know," I said.

"Look kid, where are we going?" Blue suit asked, shaking me from my thoughts.

"You guys are going to have to follow me. I'll get you to where you belong," I said to them and turned to go.

"I'm not sure Ralph; I think we should stay here," Brown suit said.

"Maybe you're right; maybe we should stay right here," Blue suit answered him, looking at me.

"I wouldn't advise that," Cadence said to them.

"Oh yeah, why not, girlie?" Blue suit said.

"I think Mr. Black is out again," she said.

"Who's this Mr. Black?" Blue suit said.

"He eats people," she answered.

Chapter 33

We finally got the two suits to follow us back to the circle. There was no sign of Manny or Mr. Black or of the Chiefs for that matter. The four of us crossed the stream and headed to the markers. I placed the camera on a marker and left it on wide angle; it was aimed at the center of the circle. We entered the ring and walked to the center.

"You guys need to hold each other's hands." I advised. They looked at me as if I insulted their mothers.

"We ain't holding hands, kid," Blue suit said defiantly. I was in no mood to play with these guys.

"OK, put your arms around each other like you're posing for a picture." I said. Contact was contact and that should suffice. They hesitated but complied.

"I can't believe we're doing this," Blue suit said.

"Me neither," Brown suit said. I needed to act fast but I felt I was missing something. The Chiefs! The last time that I had done this was when all of the Chiefs were present. I was not sure that I alone could send them home, but they were holding hands and not happy about it. I gave it a try anyway.

I closed my eyes and envisioned them going into the light; I breathed deeply and focused the pressure with my diaphragm. I felt Cadence put her hands on both of my shoulders. Though my eyelids were closed I could see the flash; the men in the suits were gone. At least I knew that I could do that by myself; I could operate the door alone.

Cadence was amazed. She wondered at the flash of light and the momentary gust of wind. "That was really cool," She smiled. I agreed; it was really cool. Someone else agreed with us as well.

"Nicely done, Chief." Manny's voice came from behind. "Thanks for opening the door for me." Cadence and I turned quickly; Manny was walking from the tree line towards us. He was sauntering, cocky in his behavior and mannerisms. We stood motionless watching him approach. Once he was close enough I saw them; those black eyes.

"Hello, Mr. Black," I said. Cadence looked to me confused but Manny applauded briefly.

"You figured that out pretty quickly, boy," Manny said. This time his voice wasn't Manny's; it was deep and gravely not unlike the voice Tony tried to scare me with. He walked up to us and I kept Cadence behind me. I wasn't sure what he was going to do or what I would have done if he attacked us.

Instead he walked passed us to the center of the circle. He bent over and removed a piece of sod from the ground revealing a shallow hole. He reached in and pulled out a stone about the size of an apple. He stood and dropped the sod then turned to us with a smug look. He tossed the rock into the air then caught it with one hand and tossed it again. Toss, catch, toss, catch.

"This is a key," he started, "and I propped the doorway open."

"I just sent those men to the light," I stated.

"Yes you did. That was a job well done." He smiled.

"What do you want Mr. Black?" Cadence asked from behind me.

"Cadence, I'm not Mr. Black. I'm still Manny; well, physically anyway. I've been taken by him as a...sort of...assistant."

"When you were in the other side." I was thinking aloud.

"Yes, on the other side." Manny was speaking deeper and louder now; he was getting angry. "Mr. Black shoved a piece of himself down my throat and it went inside of me. It grew inside of me." Tears were coming to his black eyes.

"Now he has me," Manny said, his cocky stance replaced by tearful pleading.

"Manny!" Cadence shouted. Manny's face was a conflict of emotion and for a brief time he seemed to be fighting within himself. He dropped to one knee as if his body was not in control for the moment. He dropped the stone and began clenching and unclenching his fists. He was drooling. Then he looked up to us.

"Mr. Black is coming. RUN!" Manny said in his own voice. For that one moment his eyes were back to normal. He continued his inner battle and I took the opportunity. I left the circle and led Cadence to the stream; I needed the Chiefs desperately. I could hear the roars of Mr. Black and the screams of our friend Manny behind us as he bravely fought to keep possession of himself.

We reached the stream and stopped. I looked around for the Fire Chief; I was *willing* him to appear.

He stepped out from a thicket of trees, with a look of concern on his face. He waved to us to follow him, which we were eager to do and led us down the trail in a direction we had yet to explore. The stream veered off to the right and was no longer on the side of the trail. There were more trees, a thick forest of them, and the path grew wider as we travelled.

We were walking briskly, not yet at a run. We walked for what seemed to be about a mile; Manny did not give chase. The forest opened into a meadow and there we found a primitive village of wooden structures. They were made carefully from bundles of sticks and logs, some held together by dried mud. We stopped at the edge of the village and saw the Chiefs going about their daily routines; we had reached the homes of the Chiefs.

They acted as if they weren't even aware of what was transpiring on the sacred ground of the circle.

****

I put the camera on the ground; I went to the Fire Chief and reached for his hand. He was not prepared for contact and tried to move but I was too quick and had him in my grasp. The transference took place and my mind replayed the events for him from our arrival onward. I could see the realization on his face.

I was confused as to why they somehow did not know themselves but in contacting the Fire Chief the alarm was sounded for all to hear. They dropped whatever they were doing and came to us.

I could feel them communicating with one another; they were very surprised that Mr. Black was so close to them without their knowledge. I could get bits and pieces of their communication from the transference. They were concerned for my friend Manny, they were also glad I could return the two men in suits to the light. They had no idea that the remaining townsfolk on the hill had disappeared. We all feared the worst.

I shared all of this with Cadence as I was now in the habit of holding her hand most of the time. She seemed to understand some of what was happening. The Chiefs agreed to follow us back and to meet Mr. Black head on once more as we had done before. Some had run back to gather up the sacks that they usually carried while the others began to head for the path at the tree line. We'd been in the village for only moments; but we were already leaving. I could sense Cadence's concern that we would not get back in time to help Manny.

But, we did not have to go back. All twenty-five feet of Mr. Black was coming down the pathway through the forest and heading right for us.

Chapter 34

 $\mathcal{T}$ he Chiefs stopped in their tracks and began their chant, except for the Fire Chief, who pushed me aside. When he did, I gleaned his intentions. I would not assemble with the other seven Chiefs into the Great Warrior as we had done before. I would take Cadence back to the doorway to escape while they kept Mr. Black occupied. They were certain that they could contain him even without my help.

I thought to protest but the Chiefs had assembled without me. As one, they had become a Great Warrior who was about thirty feet tall. His face was stern and his hands were clenched. He braced for a frontal assault. Mr. Black was forcing his way down the path, knocking down trees and stomping the ground beneath him. I picked up the video camera and held it in Mr. Black's general direction hoping to capture something on tape.

Once Mr. Black saw the Great Warrior he charged, roaring as he ran. They collided with a great thud and the ground shook beneath us as the battle began. Pushed back into the clearing near the village, the Great Warrior gripped Mr. Black in a bear hug.

This was our opportunity. We broke for the tree line and ran down the pathway as quickly as we could. I pulled Cadence behind me and did not dare turn around. I heard the battle continue with the thud of weight hitting the ground and the crack of trees limbs snapping.

The Chiefs then broadcast their thoughts to me and I knew that Mr. Black was coming after us. I had to look back.

He had seen us flee and had broken free. The Great Warrior reached for his legs, wrapping his massive arms around them. Mr. Black fell forward into the forest. We continued running and though we were sucking in air we could not tire; our legs did not fail us.

The further away we were, the more distant the sound of battle. The Chiefs had somehow managed to contain Mr. Black, and we were back to the stream and the markers of the sacred ground. We crossed through the water and headed out of the woods to the circle. Cadence screamed.

"Manny!" she cried. Manny was in the center of the circle lying on his back. As we approached, we could see that his eyes were closed and he wasn't breathing. I put the camera on the ground and checked his pulse; his flesh was already cold.

"Is he..." she started, but could not say the word.

"I think so," I said. Cadences' eyes were already welling with tears. I looked down to Manny and noticed that there was a slight smile on his face. I supposed that he had won his victory and bought us the time we needed with his life.

We did not have much time to mourn; there was a large crash in the forest and a roar from Mr. Black alerting us that time was short.

"We can't just leave him here!" Cadence yelled to me. Hauling Manny around would not only be difficult but it could prove fatal; he was carrying around Mr. Black inside him.

"He's contaminated. We have to."

"No!" she screamed.

I grabbed her hand and closed my eye. I tried to envision my closet, our neighborhood and our homes. Cadence was pulling away from my grip but I held her tightly. I breathed deeply and focused the pressure in my core. I had no time to cry for Manny but as I felt the world fade to black I could hear my mind say, "Goodbye."

****

We were in the closet again but the video camera was left behind. Cadence finally freed herself from me and pushed the door open. "You left him there! We have to go back." She was angry and upset, tears streaming down her face.

"I did what I thought was right," I said sounding not so sure of myself. Manny was dead, his body was trapped in another time and place.

Cadence went into the closet. "Send me back," she said.

"I can't, Cadence."

"Can't or won't," she said.

"Both," I answered. "We can't let Mr. Black get through to our world; that would be a disaster. You know that and I know that."

"You're a coward; you've abandoned your friend," she said. I certainly felt like what she was describing. I felt like I let the whole world down; maybe I had. "He's your friend and he died trying to save you, to save *us*. We have to do something." Cadence's voice was becoming smaller and less hateful; she was hurt and confused, as was I.

I grabbed her hand and said, "Come with me."

"Where are we going?"

"We're doing *something*, just like you said." I dragged her behind me, down the stairs, out of the front door toward the Blanches' house. We walked up to the stockade fence that barricaded the backyard and kept the swimming pool from being found by small children. The latch was unlocked so I lifted it and opened the gate. I closed it again once we were through.

The backyard was full of about thirty people. Some were in the pool but most were eating, drinking and talking. Some of the older men threw horseshoes in the pit; the clang of the shoes hitting the post echoed all around. Mom was sitting with several ladies in a patio chair under an umbrella; Dad was talking to Mr. Green and a few men I did not know. I made a beeline straight for Dad.

I interrupted his conversation. "Dad, can I see you for a moment?"

"You'll have to hold on for a moment," he answered.

"It's important."

"He can't help himself when he has a bee in his bonnet," said Mr. Green, whose mood seemed much improved due to an afternoon of drinking.

Dad stood up. "What did you want to tell me?"

I stepped back for a little privacy and he followed. "Something terrible has happened; Manny is stuck on the other side and he might be dead. The Chiefs..." I started, but Dad cut me off.

"Hold on, what happened to Manny?".

"We went to the Chiefs and we..." Dad cut me off again.

"Oh, come on. Can we do this later? Can't you kids do something until the cookout is over?"

"I said that it was important!"

Dad stopped and looked at me; some other people looked our way briefly but returned to their own activity after a moment. Dad then looked to Cadence and I could see something register in his eyes when he looked at her. Her eyes were red and puffy, tears still shined on her face. He knew then that we weren't playing around. Mr. Blanche was watching from the grill and I also noticed Mr. Green showing alarm on his face as well.

Mr. Topaz came up from behind me and asked, "What's going on?"

"I don't know," Dad started, "but I think something's happened at our house that the kids want to show us. Bill, Alvin, would you mind following me and the kids next door? Let's do this quietly so we don't upset anyone."

"Looks like these two are plenty upset already," Mr. Topaz said.

"Excuse us, fellas," Mr. Green said to the men I did not know.

We left the backyard and marched over to our house. Cadence was calmer now that something was being done. I think the presence of the adults helped. We reached our porch and we stopped.

"OK, what happened?" Dad asked.

This was it. I was going to have to reveal everything including the existence of Mr. Black. One obstacle was convincing them that something had happened to Manny. The biggest hurdle, the trick to the whole thing, was convincing them to come with us to the other side.

Chapter 35

I must admit, the three adults were patient. I started retelling the tale of going to see the Chiefs and about the people on the hill, about Joe and Tony. I told them about the ceremony and the stone markers and then about Mr. Black. Towards the end of my story, Dad was trying to look apologetic to Mr. Topaz and Mr. Green, but they listened and asked appropriate questions when needed.

"That's quite a story," my father said.

"Of all people, Dad, you should be the one to believe it. You saw Tony yourself," I said.

"Show me the closet," Mr. Green said. We all looked at each other for a moment then I led them inside. We crammed into my bedroom and I showed them the open closet with the scratches covering the back side of the door. The clothes were still hung neatly and shoes lined the back wall.

Dad stood with his hands on his hips. Maybe he didn't want to believe. He was definitely in denial. Mr. Green stepped into the closet and was followed by Mr. Topaz who held out his hand.

"You gonna leave me hanging?" Mr. Topaz asked. I grasped his hand and followed them in, Cadence behind me.

"Dad, are you coming?" I asked peering out from behind the door.

"What the hell," he answered and followed us in. It was nearly impossible for all of us to fit in there. I just knew that my good shoes were being trampled. I heard the metal hangars scraping against the rod as the clothes were forced to make room for the people.

"Close the door," I said and Dad pulled it shut. Cadence gripped my hand so hard it hurt. I hadn't expected to return so soon after finding Manny in the circle. I was more scared that Mr. Black would be waiting for us. I forced myself to concentrate and pictured the scene. I closed my eyes and breathed deeply, forcing the energy from my midsection.

"Now what?" Dad asked.

It was working; I could smell the grass and feel the breeze. The darkness of the closet was lifting slowly. I opened my eyes and tensed for some kind of confrontation but all I saw was the growing brightness of a cloudy day. The grass was beneath my feet and the clouds above us did not appear that ominous.

"Remarkable," I heard Mr. Green say in almost a whisper.

"Holy cow! Now we know how their names got on that rock," Mr. Topaz added.

"I can explain," I began but they were too enthralled with the place to listen. We let go of each other and I looked down expecting to see Manny's body on the ground. But, he was gone, as was Mr. Black. That was the good news. More good news was that the video camera was still where I'd left it. The bad news was that my father did not make the trip with us.

"Where's my Dad?" I asked to the group. We looked around but he wasn't there.

"He may have been left behind." Mr. Green guessed. I hoped he was right. Why hadn't Dad make the trip with us? I had no way of knowing.

"So where's Manny?" Mr. Topaz asked. They were taking this rather well and that was throwing me off of my game.

"He should be right here," I said pointing to the ground. They gathered in the area Manny was before we had gone home the first time.

I went over to the video camera. It was off; the battery was dead, but it seemed undamaged. The tape had recorded almost to the end, so what happened to Manny could have been captured by the camera. Since I couldn't recharge it, I left it on my own stone marker for the time being. I turned to my father's two friends.

"Have you guys been here before?" I asked them. Cadence looked at me with that question; she seemed confused as well.

"No, but we know someone who had," Mr. Topaz responded without looking up. My hunch was somewhat correct; they were familiar with this place!

"You should explain," I said to Mr. Topaz.

"Greeny will do that; I'm going to have a look around," Mr. Topaz said as he walked to the edge of the circle. Mr. Green was scanning the area but he had heard what Mr. Topaz had said to us.

"I have a diary," Mr. Green began as he walked the circle, "that belonged to thirteen-year-old Julia Atkins. It begins on March 25, 1867. It was part of the donation to the Society by the Atkins family when they sold the farm in the 1950s. In it, she describes the place on her farm that eventually becomes your neighborhood. According to the diary, she spent many days there escaping from her tyrannical father.

"She described a vision of an Indian Chief not unlike the ones you yourself have described. From time to time, in the woods behind her house, the Indian Chief would appear. They would never speak but she would have strange dreams about him. She had written that she was afraid of the Chief and that he would somehow take her away to his world. Still, she continued to return to this portion of her farm."

"Her last entry included a trip to this world. She called it a 'trip down the rabbit's hole,' just like the *Alice in Wonderland* story. She wrote about the circle of markers. She returned home but never wrote in the diary again. She subsequently moved to an aunt's house in Boston."

When Mr. Green finished, we were standing at my stone marker.

"What happened to her after that?" Cadence asked.

"Oh, she married and moved away. I don't think she returned often to the farm, if ever," Mr. Green said, as he looked at the stone. I looked to the next marker where Mr. Topaz was standing. He was staring into the tree line towards the stream.

"Alvin, take a look!" Mr. Topaz exclaimed. We all looked in that direction and saw the Fire Chief fast approaching. He walked right up to me and placed his right hand on my left shoulder and my right hand on his. The transference took place with the others watching.

They had forced Mr. Black back through the doorway but Manny went with him. They were not sure if our Manny was dead but Mr. Black was in full control of him physically. The new problem was that Manny had one of the keys to the doorway; the stone talisman he had been carrying. The marker on it was a smaller version of the man with four arms.

Up to now, Mr. Black was limited in travel to the astral planes. He could not go to the physical world, to our world. The Chief was concerned that with the help of Manny's body and this talisman, Mr. Black could travel to the physical world. If time was meaningless beyond the physical, as it seemed to be in this realm, then in theory, they could appear anytime.

The one positive point was that with the talisman, they would be limited to the same physical place as the circle of markers. But this meant that they could appear in my yard, at my house, anytime. Not to mention me, but Mom and Dad would definitely not like having a twenty-five foot creature stomping around the place. We might not know when, but at least we knew where they could appear.

The Chief removed his hand from my shoulders and turned to Mr. Green. Holding my hand, he then repeated his action with Mr. Green, allowing me to learn what Mr. Green knew. The Chief learned the tale of Julia Atkins just as Mr. Green had told it minutes before, but Mr. Green had left out a number of details.

I learned that the Chief in Julia Atkins' diary was very young, not much older than she was at the time. His face was painted black, and he wore breechcloth and leggings with slipper like moccasins. His hair was black, straight and very long. On his bare torso was a breastplate made of bone and hide. Though he carried no weapons, he was menacing and young Julia was terrified. I saw these images in my mind. I felt them.

The Chief finished with Mr. Green and gestured to us to join him in the center of the circle. He sat on the ground and we copied him. Mr. Green, being the oldest of the group, had difficulty getting down on the ground, but Mr. Topaz helped him. The Fire Chief meditated.

"You are a Fire Chief," Mr. Green said to me. "So was he."

"Who was a Fire Chief?" Cadence asked.

"The Chief Julia Atkins wrote about in her diary," Mr. Green answered.

"Which one was he?" Cadence asked.

"He isn't one of the eight Chiefs," Mr. Green began, "he's another one."

Chapter 36

$\mathcal{I}$ placed my hand on the Chief's hand and the images quickly flooded my mind. I was a Chief, one of them and yet I was not. I focused on the questions at hand and heard myself asking the Chief verbally yet not aloud. "Where are the people that were on the hill the last time we were here?"

"We are not sure but believe that they are gone, taken by Mr. Black." His voice was like a thousand voices, speaking as one, like being in the school auditorium when we all recited the Pledge of Allegiance.

"Are they taken as hostages or helpers?" I asked.

"We cannot be sure" was the response.

"Were they eaten?"

"We do not know. A lost one cannot be eaten as their bodies are already gone; in the act their spirits are consumed and lost forever."

"Who is the other Chief? The one Mr. Green learned of in the diary of the Atkins girl," I asked.

"He was to be the eighth Chief, a Fire Chief. He was chosen young, like you. He broke the laws of the tribe and our gods; he was cast out."

"What law did he break?"

"He killed an innocent."

"Whom did he kill?"

"A woman who was to be his wife; she loved another."

"How was he so young? What happened to him that he did not age?" I continued.

"He died that very night by the hands of her father; so he is forever young. He was buried alone; far from the burial grounds so that he would continue to be punished even in death. In death he found this place," the Fire Chief said.

"What did he do then?"

"He cursed at us, tried to stop us from helping the lost ones. Then we were attacked by the Evil One and he was taken below."

"Is this other Chief the Mr. Black that Joe spoke of?"

"Yes."

"Then who is the Evil One that took him?"

"There are many below; the Evil One is their Chief. The Evil One gives the shadow demons their power. The shadow demons were ready to receive, already possessed by their hatred and anger."

"How many are there?"

"We do not know."

I broke contact with the Chief and watched him for a moment. He looked to me with a knowing smile. This was his plan when we sat; to draw us in close so that I could get this information from him. I let go and the Chief instructed me to share the information with the others. I asked Mr. Green and Mr. Topaz and Cadence to circle around me and hold hands.

"Son, I don't think we have to time to sit around and hold hands right now," Mr. Green said.

"Greeny, let the kid hold our hands if he wants to make himself feel better."

Cadence held Step's hand and Mr. Green took her hand and Mr. Topaz took Step's. The circle closed, and Step began to transfer the information the Chief had shared with him. Cadence, who greatly feared the unknown, seemed even more alarmed.

We all knew that even if we could defeat Mr. Black, another would take his place. The sense of dread was shared by all. I suddenly appreciated the job that the eight Chiefs had, and realized the importance of the job I would have, the job I did have.

"What happens if we find the burial site of Mr. Black?" I asked.

"How could we do that?" Cadence asked. How indeed.

"We could ask the Chiefs if they know the location. Then we could use the maps at the Historical Society to triangulate the spot in our world." I was thinking aloud.

"What good will that do?" Mr. Topaz said.

"I'm not sure; I don't know if it will do any good at all. I'm not sure of the Namtuxet dogma; I'm not the most fluent in Christian dogma either. But the importance of his burial location is nagging at me," I said. I stood up, wiping off my pants.

"Bury him in holy ground," Mr. Green said almost to himself. I heard him well enough.

"Yes, that could be it. We need to exhume him and relocate the remains to holy ground," I said. Things were beginning to click in my mind, to come together like pieces of a puzzle.

"You're going to bury him in your yard?" Cadence asked. Good question; bad idea, I thought.

"No, we can't bury him there; that's the doorway. That would probably worsen the situation," I said.

"We could bury him behind the church," Mr. Green said, completely on board.

I sat again and touched the Fire Chief's hand. "Where is his body buried?"

＊＊＊＊

"We need to go home now," I said to the group.

"Yes, I'm sure that they are missing us next door at the cookout," Mr. Topaz added.

"What about Manny?" Cadence asked. We stopped and looked to each other.

"I'm sorry sweetheart," Mr. Green said as gently as possible. "Manny is gone and we have no way of finding him."

Cadence was again a mixture of anger, resentment and loss. She did not even try to hide the tears that followed.

"We may be able to find him if we can somehow locate Mr. Black and subdue him," I said trying to give her some hope, of which I had very little. "We'll review the video; maybe it will show us something."

We stood; Mr. Topaz again helped Mr. Green to his feet. The Fire Chief stood with us and placed one hand on my shoulder, looking into my eyes. He was grave. I could feel his hopes going with us. He left the circle and watched us from beyond the stone markers. With my camera in one hand and Cadence's hand in the other, I closed my eyes and began my thought process again. Breathing deeply I focused the pressure on my midsection. The light of day began to fade.

Mr. Green had one arm around Cadence and the other around Mr. Topaz. They were all sharing Cadence's emotional outpouring over the fate of our friend Manny. No sooner did the light fade when I felt shirts and suits draped against my back. We had returned to my dark closet. Mr. Topaz opened the door and flooded it with light.

"I thought you'd already come out of one of these," Mr. Topaz quipped to Mr. Green.

"Bill, a comedian you are not," Mr. Green replied, the mood a bit lightened. Next out was Cadence and then I followed. Our small group stood there in front of Dad, who was sitting on my bed.

"That was fast," he said. He was wide eyed at the sight of us.

"How long were we gone?" Mr. Topaz asked.

"About five minutes," Dad said.

"How come you didn't go with us?" Mr. Topaz asked.

"I have no idea. We were crammed in there together then there was a bright flash of light and the next thing I know I was alone. I opened the door and sat on the bed to wait."

I was unsure why Dad could not pass with the rest of us. I was trying to remember what Joe had told us. There were no rules, time had no meaning and you had to want to go; you had to believe. Maybe Dad was too scared to go. I would have to think about it some more later.

"I don't see Manny. What did you find?" Dad asked.

"Mr. Green or Mr. Topaz can fill you in while I load up this tape. I need to see if I can find anything that will help us," I said as I made my way to the stairs. Cadence followed me, and the adults stayed in my room, their voices deep and sober.

I went to the living room and turned on the television and VCR; I pushed in the tape and pressed 'rewind.'

The three men came down into the living room. The tape reached the beginning and I pressed "play." All eyes were on the screen. The image was shaky and snowy, but I adjusted the tracking and it cleared somewhat. On the tape, even the slightest breeze sounded like a whipping wind. First I filmed us were in the circle; then I filmed all eight markers. At its position next to my leg, the camera jostled quite a bit during our long walk.

Anyone else would be hard pressed to tell where we actually were. It was green and there were trees. It could have been anywhere except for the stone markers. The video replayed our long walk to the hill and our meeting with the men in the suits.

"Who are they?" Dad asked.

"They are lost; we will get them home," I answered.

"Home, where?" he asked again.

"Just watch Dad," I said.

The men in the suits were walking with us for quite some time until we were again back at the circle. They argued with us about holding hands, but soon had their arms around each other's shoulders, as if posed for a picture. That's when I'd placed the camera on a stone so Cadence and I could also be seen in the shot. Everyone looked small because the camera was on wide angle.

"I really want to see this," Mr. Green said.

One minute the men in the suits were standing there and then there was a bright light. The camera's lens couldn't handle the light so the whole screen went white briefly. Then the men were gone and all we could see was the circle again. We heard Cadence's voice say, "That was really cool."

We all froze when Manny said, "Nicely done, Chief." Manny entered the screen. We relived our dialog with Manny. We watched as he pulled the talisman out of his hiding spot in the ground. He tossed it in the air and argued with us. Then he dropped to one knee, and yelled, "RUN!" again. Our images ran out of the frame.

This was the part I wanted to see. Nothing happened. I could hear Manny breathing heavily off screen. Then a bright light appeared. Mr. Black could be seen climbing out of a hole in the ground that had not been there seconds before, and once he was out, the hole disappeared. He towered over Manny, who cowered beneath him. And then Manny flew back, knocked to the ground, and appeared to be out cold. A hit that hard could have killed him. Mr. Black stormed off the screen.

"What was that?" Mr. Topaz yelled.

"That was Mr. Black," I answered.

Chapter 37

$\mathcal{T}$he video seemed still. Manny just lay there. Cadence and I entered the frame and determined that Manny was gone and it was time to go. A bright light flashed and we were gone. Manny sat bolt upright then walked out of the circle, out of view.

"Where is he going?" Cadence asked.

"I don't know but I'm pretty sure that he's not dead," Mr. Topaz offered.

"Who exactly is Mr. Black?" Dad said nervously.

We told Dad everything, including the fact that Mr. Black was capable of invading our time, our property and our lives.

The camera's battery died shortly after Manny left the screen. I stopped the video and rewound the tape while my father, Mr. Green and Mr. Topaz again discussed the content.

"What do we do now?" Cadence asked.

The men looked up and paused.

"We go back next door and make an appearance at the cookout. We've been gone about twenty minutes. I think I need a drink," Dad answered.

"What about Manny?" Cadence asked, and I could see tears welling up in her eyes. She was getting upset again.

"Manny seems to be alright for the time being. After all, he did get up and walk away," Mr. Green said. "But we'll have to prepare to go back for him. I'll go to the hall to research the location of Mr. Black's remains."

"I'll join you," Mr. Topaz said. They told us they would return as soon as they found some answers, and they left in Mr. Green's car.

Dad went back to the cookout, but Cadence was still too upset to be with so many people. She and I stayed at my house and sat on the couch holding each other.

****

Only an hour later, Mr. Green and Mr. Topaz returned. Mom and Dad were still next door and Cadence was asleep on the couch. I was sitting at the kitchen table doing my calculus homework when I let them.

"What did you find?" I whispered, so I wouldn't wake Cadence.

"We know where Mr. Black is buried," Mr. Green said, as he spread out a map on the table over my work.

"Where?"

"The high school of all places," Mr. Topaz said. Mr. Green pulled out a copy of an old town map from the previous century. Using the description that the Fire Chief provided he found the area and marked it in pencil. Before he showed the modern map I could already see familiar landmarks that placed the high school where the mark was.

"How are we going to exhume the remains from the high school?" I asked.

"Take a closer look at the newer map," Mr. Green said. The marking was at the south end of the high school where the football field was.

"It's near the football field," I said. This was not my high school but I was familiar with it; Dad would sometimes take us to sporting events there.

"Correct. Now let me show you this map of the campus," Mr. Green said, producing a larger map of the high school and surrounding area in great detail.

The mark on this map was where the bleachers were now, near the edge of the property by the chain-link fence. A small stream ran behind the property. Two streets intersected behind the school property in the shape of a pie wedge.

"Long before the homes were built, the area was farmland, and the roads travelled by horses and farm animals," Mr. Topaz said.

"Where exactly is the site?" I asked.

And then I could picture exactly where it had to be. At the entrance to a path in the woods behind the school, there was a large rock that looked like a cube or a boundary marker. Kids would sit hang out back there, and it was often the meeting site for kids who were skipping class. I had seen this rock myself, and I was sure Mr. Topaz had too. In his days as a police officer, he'd probably told a hundred kids to get up from there and get to school.

Over the years, the rock had been almost covered with kids' initials marked in spray paint or nicked with knives. If any Namtuxet markings were on it, deciphering them from all the others would be almost impossible.

"I know that rock," I said.

Mr. Topaz smiled and said, "I didn't think that *you* would hang out there."

"I never did but I've seen it."

"Either way, the stone is hidden in both directions, by the trees and by the football bleachers. It's still very risky but we could dig there at night," Mr. Green said.

"I told you, Alvin, I've got this covered. We won't have to lift a shovel; I have someone on the inside," Mr. Topaz confided.

"Who is going to do all the digging on the inside?" Mr. Green mocked Mr. Topaz.

"I know the groundskeepers very well. As a matter of fact, they all owe me favors."

"Oh?" Mr. Green prodded him on. I was curious as well.

"Back in the days when I wore the uniform and those fine, upstanding citizens were young I had them as... clients let's just say."

"Clients?"

Mr. Topaz took a moment to look sternly at Mr. Green. "They've all been in trouble with the law, a couple of them more than once. I helped them out during those trying times so like I said; they owe me favors."

"What do you propose?" Mr. Green asked.

"They take the backhoe over there and dig. They've been talking about putting in boulders to keep kids on dirt bikes from cutting through the path and ruining the football field anyway," Mr. Topaz said. "I'll just let them know we're looking for historical artifacts. If they find anything they'll call me, and no one else. I pick you up and we go there, put the remains in my trunk and drive away. They fill in the hole and put their boulders to block the path and no one is the wiser."

"These groundskeepers won't talk?" Mr. Green asked.

"No, these fellas owe me and I think that they'll make it square. They won't talk," Mr. Topaz assured us.

"When can they start?" I asked.

"I'll swing by Tommy's now, he's head groundskeeper. I busted him about twenty years ago on a breaking and entering with the Gelb boy. Since it was their first time, I took them home to their folks. Mr. Gelb messed his son up pretty good for that and he was never a problem again. Tommy got popped for shoplifting a couple of times after that but he outgrew all that; I helped him get that job for the town. Tommy will arrange it. Since it's Monday it will probably be the day after tomorrow. I'll let you all know."

Mr. Topaz and Mr. Green stood to leave.

"I'll tell my Dad."

"Good, I'll leave the maps for him," Mr. Green said.

"Please tell Cadence I was asking for her when she wakes up," Mr. Topaz said as he shook my hand and smiled at me. I smiled back. It was the first time I had ever shaken his hand; it was also the last.

Chapter 38

*L*ater that night, long after Cadence had gone home, my father was reviewing the maps that Mr. Green had left for him and Mom was getting ready for bed. They were both tired from a day in the sun with too much food and drink. And I was exhausted from our trip to the other side.

I went through my nightly ritual. I said goodnight to my parents, brushed my teeth and put on my pajamas. And, I'd recently added one more step to my nightly routine: I put on the crucifix, which I'd received for my First Communion, which I wore on a chain around my neck. I was neatly tucked in bed by nine o'clock and was asleep within minutes.

I awoke to the sound of someone banging on the closet door. I sat upright, and reached for the flashlight, but I'd returned it to the garage. The door opened and I expected to see Tony again, but another figure stepped out. I turned on the bedside lamp and its soft light shown on Manny's face as he looked at me from the closet door.

"Manny?" I asked.

"Yes and no," Manny answered. "Manny is in here with me. Say 'Hello' Manny." His face distorted and the deeper voice was replaced by Manny's own.

"Hey kid, don't worry about me. Kick this bad guy's butt!"

"Oh, I doubt very much that he can do that," the deeper voice said.

"Leave Manny alone," I said in an even tone. I was on the bed on my knees ready to bolt at any moment.

"No," Manny's deeper voice replied.

"What do you want?"

"To open the doorway for my friend Mr. Black. You were very difficult to find, you know."

"No, he is not welcome here."

"He's already on his way. All I need to do is bring this talisman to his stone marker and, thanks to you, I now know where it is."

"DAD!" I screamed.

"They cannot help you; no one can," the deeper voice said.

But I heard heavy footsteps coming down the hall. Dad appeared at the door and was startled to see Manny.

"Manny, are you alright?" Dad asked.

"Dad, that is not Manny," I blurted.

"Yes 'Dad,' Manny is here with me. He's quite well, I assure you," the deeper voice said.

With that, Dad was gone from the doorway, his footsteps fast on the stairs. "Even your father is afraid of me," he said.

"I'm not afraid of you," I said. But I wondered why my father took off like that.

"Maybe not, but you will be. I'll get you, your friends and your family. I'll watch you all die. We'll start with your girlfriend Cadence and save you for last, so you can watch."

When he said Cadence's name, something in me snapped and I leapt from the bed and tackled Manny to the ground. But, his strength was superhuman. He threw me aside as if I were a ragdoll. I recovered and pounced on him again, wrapping my arms around his neck and squeezing as hard as I could. I had never been in a fight before but I'd watched enough movies to have some idea of attack in mind.

He forced me from his shoulders and I fell to the floor. Even in the dim light I could see evil in his black eyes. Still, he did not come for me so I stood and went at him again. Again he tossed me aside. I was just a plaything to him. He was unstoppable. I tried one last time, wrapping myself around him in a bear hug, and he did not resist.

He stood with me wrapped around him and walked to the bedroom door. He continued down the stairs unimpaired, as if I wasn't even there. I could hear Mom stirring in the bedroom from all of the noise. Dad was by the phone in the living room when he saw us, and he ran over to help.

"Manny stay here. I'm getting you help," Dad said.
Manny back-handed him, launching Dad backwards onto the couch
and then he flung me from his shoulders and headed to the door.

Mom screamed from the top of the stairs, "What is going
on?"

As Manny opened the door, we heard the screeching tires of
a car outside. Mr. Topaz appeared at the door breathing heavily and
yelled, "Manny!"

Manny ran.

My father was wiping blood from his lip, split and bleeding.

"He's going for the stone marker at the school," I said. "He
says he has some talisman that will open the doorway for
that...thing, Mr. Black."

"You two throw something on and chase him down," Mr.
Topaz said. "I'll go get Alvin and we'll get over to the high school.
Tommy told me where the key to the backhoe is but I'll have to
break the lock on the school storage building where they keep it."

"You're going to dig now?" my father asked. Mom came
down the stairs and ran to Dad's side, trying to wipe his lip.

"Looks like we have to; unless you want that giant, black
monster running around eating people," Mr. Topaz said.

"Was that Manny in our house at this hour?" Mom asked.

"Yes Mom," I said on my way up the stairs. I grabbed some
shoes and a coat from my bedroom. I could hear Dad behind me,
running to dress too.

"Where do you two think you're going?" Mom asked
bewildered at the activity around her.

"To save Manny," I said. "Hurry up, Dad!" I yelled.

I thought Mom would have put up more of an argument, but
she must have been so concerned for Manny that our leaving didn't
seem extraordinary. As we were leaving she only said, "Be careful."
Then she watched us get in the car and back out of the driveway.

Dad raced down the street and it didn't take us long to find Manny in a light jog in the middle of the road. He'd heard us coming and stepped aside to let us by. Dad drove ahead of him then pulled over. He stopped the engine and took the keys from the ignition. As I got out I pulled the crucifix from my neck and held it tight in my hand.

"Oh, it's you," Many said coming to a stop. He had gone about a mile and wasn't even breathing hard.

"Manny, come home with us," Dad pleaded.

"Don't you know who I am?" Manny asked incredulously. "We are the Dark Ones, the Shadow Man, Mr. Black, Herr Dunkle, Giza Moja...we have a thousand names," Manny said spreading his arms wide.

"Manny, we can help you. Get in the car, son," Dad continued.

"I am not the one who needs help; you are," he said before breaking into a sprint, heading straight for my father. Manny slammed his full weight at Dad and sent him flying. He came down hard on the pavement and was lucky enough not to hit his head. Then Manny came for me and I swung the fist that was clutching the crucifix. My hand felt like it connected with a cement wall. Manny had not only stopped; he was staggering backwards. But, he recovered quickly and looked even angrier and charged again. I swung the same fist into his gut and heard him grunt with an *oooff* sound. He was slowed, certainly, but he was still driven to harm me. It was his turn to connect his fist with my head and I instantly saw stars. I staggered back and fell against the car. I couldn't focus on anything, but I heard my Dad take on Manny again and again Dad hit the ground. Then I heard Manny's footsteps as he jogged away.

We slowed him but we could not stop him.

Manny was running at a brisk pace with only one more mile to go before the school. Time was definitely not on our side. Mr. Topaz had to stop and pick up Mr. Green, drive to the school, break into the storage building, start the backhoe and move it to the stone marker near the football field, and then dig and exhume a body. After all that he needed to take the remains to the Church and bury it all before Manny could place the talisman on the stone marker.

My head was pounding, but I was able to function again. Dad also recovered and waved me back into the car. He fired it up and we were back on our way. Another half mile down the road, we came upon Manny again. I wanted Dad to run Mr. Black down but we would hurt Manny too.

"You know, we'll have to do that again," Dad did not sound very positive.

"If that's what it takes." I said. We pulled ahead of him and stopped, this time Dad left the Lincoln running. We got out of the car and Manny was already charging us. Dad paid dearly as Manny connected with him first; I heard a crunch and hoped it wasn't a breaking bone. Dad dropped to the ground; he was down for the count.

I had the crucifix in my hand and jumped Manny from behind as he stood laughing over my father. This time, I slipped the crucifix in his pants pocket before he flung me over his shoulder and was off again, leaving Dad and me beside the road.

Dad's breathing was labored. He tried to sit up.

"I think I broke a rib," he said.

"Get in the back seat, Dad. I'll get us there."

"You can't drive."

"Well you can't, and I know enough about driving to get us there."

"I guess we don't have much of a choice. Are you sure Step?"

"Don't worry Dad."

He struggled to sit up and get to his feet. I tried to help but Dad outweighed me by at least fifty pounds. I opened the rear door and he slid himself across the seat.

I hopped into the driver's seat and stepped on the brake. I slid the gear selector to drive then let go of the brake; I eased the gas. We began to roll. I kept our speed to about 25 miles per hour and headed for the high school. I was so grateful that we didn't see another car on the road.

Finally, we arrived at the high school.

Chapter 39

I pulled into the parking lot, my headlights aimed at the tennis courts. I shut off the lights and the motor, but I left the keys in the ignition for my father. Dad was conscious but he couldn't move even slightly without groaning.

"I'll be right back, Dad," I said to him as I got out.

"Wait, I'm coming with you."

"No Dad, don't worry. You stay."

"Promise me you'll find Bill and Alvin before you do anything," he said. "And Step? Be careful!"

I went towards the chain-link fence that led to the football field. The fence itself was eight-feet tall but the gate, though it was locked, was only six feet. I climbed the gate and hopped down, then jogged across the track towards the bleachers. I could hear the diesel engine of a backhoe, and could see its headlights moving. If the police didn't show up, it would be a miracle.

The headlights shone towards the marker stone, and standing in front of it was Manny. He stared at the stone unmoving. At his feet, Mr. Green lay on the ground. Mr. Topaz seemed to be digging perilously close to them, but he handled the machine as if he'd had plenty of experience.

I ran to Mr. Green and helped him to his feet.

"Look," Mr. Green said, pointing to the graffiti covered marker that held Manny's gaze. On it was a small statue of a man with four arms, the stone talisman that was the key to Mr. Black's power. I approached Manny, who stood there like a mannequin, his black eyes staring blankly through me. At least he was breathing.

Mr. Green and I gently pulled Manny back from the stone marker and out of the way of the backhoe. I went to the marker to remove the talisman but it would not budge, as if secured by some unseen force. If he wasn't already here, Mr. Black would soon be on his way and Manny would be discarded like an obsolete tool. The job was done.

Mr. Topaz seemed adept with the backhoe, because the hole at the base of the marker was already a few feet deep. Mr. Green pulled a flashlight from his back pocket and I could see the rich, brown earth and the roots of the trees. We both began looking through the soft dirt already piled up from the dig.

Mr. Topaz started a new pile, and on the second scoop, I saw what looked like roots. I jumped up and waved into the headlights of the backhoe for Mr. Topaz to stop. He did and leapt down from the machine to join us. I wasn't sure but I thought I knew what they were.

"Found something?" he asked. I reached down and pulled out a bone from the pile. It was a humerus, the bone that runs from the shoulder to the elbow. Mr. Topaz waved Mr. Green over.

"At least now we know this is the place," Mr. Topaz shouted over the rattling diesel engine. Mr. Green aimed the flashlight into the hole and reached down. He pulled out a skull. We all looked at each other for a minute, and all I could think was a year ago, I'd never have pictured myself here at the back of the high school, digging up a skeleton with a couple of old guys from the historical society. But now it seemed so normal.

We investigated further, and found some kind of a blanket. We started to brush the dirt off of it carefully, because we knew what we would find. Knowing sure didn't make it any easier to pull the edge of the blanket back and uncover a body.

The blanket wrapping was giving way with the slightest touch. Mr. Green told us to wait a minute, and he disappeared from the light, returning moment later with a large bed sheet and duct tape. We pulled the wrapped remains onto the bed sheet, wrapped the sheet around it, and then duct tapes the sheet together so it would not open on its own.

Mr. Green and I carried the body to the storage building on the other side of the bleachers. Mr. Topaz had parked his Ford on the grass and the trunk was open, its contents an array of bolt cutters, a shovel, pry bars and other tools the unlikely elderly duo probably used to get into the gate. We placed the remains into the trunk on top of the pile.

"Where's your Dad?" Mr. Green asked.

"He's hurt, in the backseat of our car in the parking lot."

"What happened?"

"Manny and he had a run in, back down the road. Manny wasn't himself," I said. Mr. Green stood there, rubbing his stomach, remembering his own run-in with Manny.

"It looks like you slowed him down," I said.

"Maybe, but apparently not enough."

We closed the trunk and were returning to the dig when we heard a sound over the loud diesel engine. It was an angry cry and it was very large and very close to us. Small trees toppled and the ground reverberated with each step as Mr. Black entered the scene, the hole by Mr. Topaz almost refilled. Grabbing the large backhoe's scoop, Mr. Black struggled to hold the hydraulic arm. But Mr. Topaz eased the machine forward, pushing Mr. Black backwards.

I grabbed Manny, still in a comatose state and pulled him out of harm's way. I could see Mr. Topaz in the operator's compartment of the backhoe working the controls intensely. He looked to us and I could barely make out what he said but I understood, "Get out of here! Now!"

I led Manny back to the Ford. But Mr. Green stayed in place. "Bill will be killed!" he cried.

"We all will, if we don't bury these bones in the churchyard! Please Mr. Green, we need you!" I called back to him. But I kept going. I was fully prepared to drive there myself. I felt almost as strong as I thought Manny felt, and my fortitude surprised me.

We finally reached the Ford and I pushed Manny into the backseat. He lay across the front seat not unlike my father in the backseat of the Lincoln.

Mr. Green caught up to us and got into the driver's seat. I sat in back with my father as we sped away, burning rubber much like I'd seen the high school seniors do as they left. We raced for the Lady of the Rosary Catholic Church less than a mile away. It was only a minute or two later when we arrived. Mr. Green pulled into the parking lot and headed for the back of the Church. There was a large grass lawn and behind that was Mount Olive Cemetery.

We got out of the car and Mr. Green opened the trunk.

"You're a lot younger and stronger than I am; you should start to dig. I'll gather the remains together and bring them over to you," Mr. Green said.

"Where?" I asked.

"Right there," Mr. Green said pointing to the statue of St. Mary in the center of the back lawn of the church. I took the shovel from the trunk and jogged to the statue. I went to the backside and started digging. I had only moved a dozen shovels full when I felt a familiar vibration in the ground.

Mr. Green was almost to me with the remains, "Keep digging! Get those bones into the ground!" He put them down then headed back to the car. I did as ordered; but I looked up and could see that Mr. Black was turning the corner and heading our way.

Just as Mr. Black came into the churchyard, the Ford's engine started. The car's lights came to life and it peeled out of the parking lot like a rocket and head straight between me and Mr. Black. Mr. Black came to a stop and headed towards the car. Mr. Green had bought me some time.

I continued digging.

I saw a police car fly by the church with the blue lights flashing. I could hear racing motors and screeching tires in the distance and still I continued to dig.

I dug as fast as I could to make the hole big and deep enough to hold the skeleton. It wasn't uniform but it was probably shin deep all around. I stood in it and continued scooping when I felt the ground tremble again. Mr. Black had passed the car and was heading my way. I stopped digging and went for the bed sheet. I didn't look to Mr. Black; I just kept working.

I picked up the remains; they were amazingly light, and I deposited them into the hole. I picked up the shovel and began to cover it with the dirt from my pile. This was show time; if this did not work I couldn't imagine what would. Mr. Black batted off Mr. Green's Ford again. I knew how much Mr. Topaz loved that car, and thought for a moment of the sacrifice he was making for me. I had more than half of the remains covered and I was scooping furiously.

I felt a hand on my shoulder and I screamed.

Chapter 40

Father McLaughlin had heard the commotion from the rectory on the other side of the church; he came over to investigate. He was dressed all in black with his white collar and no coat. A string of rosary beads was around his neck with a small crucifix hanging from it. He approached me just as Mr. Black was within striking distance.

"What in heaven's name is that?" he asked. As if to answer him, the gigantic figure bellowed into the night. Father McLaughlin did not flinch but instead took the beads from around his neck and began to massage them in his hand; his mouth moved with whispered prayer.

It was psalms 23:4 and I recognized it: "Yea, though I walk through the valley of the shadow of death, I will fear no evil for thou art with me; thy rod and thy staff they comfort me." Mr. Black stopped and looked at us as if deciding what to do with us. Father McLaughlin had forgotten me and started towards Mr. Black.

I looked at the hole and the partially covered remains; only about two square feet of the bed sheet was still exposed. As the Father continued to pray I shoveled ferociously. In several more scoops, the remains were covered.

Mr. Black came out of his trance and reached for Father McLaughlin, grasping him in one hand and raising him towards his mouth. Just then, a light appeared from behind Mr. Black and blinded me. I could hear the racing motor and knew that it was Mr. Green again. Mr. Green rammed the big Ford into Mr. Black causing him to stumble and drop Father McLaughlin.

With the lights knocked out from the impact I could see that the Father was on the ground but uninjured. The string of rosary beads was still in his hands. I shoveled faster, only a couple of scoops to go. Mr. Black stood and bellowed again; the Ford backed away possibly to ram him again.

With the final scoop the sheet was no longer visible, I kept shoveling anyway. Mr. Black let out the loudest cry I had heard from him as if he was in agony. My hands had grown blisters and ached from the frenzied work but I still scooped some more. I looked up to Mr. Black who was standing motionless, frozen and silent.

Mr. Black began to shrink. It was slow at first but his size diminished more quickly the smaller he became. As he shrank his appearance changed as well. Where he was once completely featureless, now human eyes appeared, then a nose and mouth. He was once again becoming the Eighth Chief who'd been cast out. He had long black hair and wore the leggings, tunic and moccasins of the Namtuxet people I'd seen in paintings. Compared to the other Chiefs, he was so young barely twenty years old if I had to guess.

Father McLaughlin went to him and stood before him. I dropped my shovel and joined them. The car door opened and Mr. Green approached. Mr. Black, now the Fire Chief, looked in Father McLaughlin's eyes as if to say something. Then he looked to me and I was not sure but it looked like the corner of his mouth went up in a smile. He began to fade and quickly disappeared as if he was made up of smoke. Father McLaughlin turned to me.

"Alright, what was all this?" he asked.

"You won't believe it Father," I said to him.

"After what I just saw, I'll believe anything. Start at the beginning."

"We can't; we don't have time," Mr. Green interjected.

"Why not? Mr. Black is gone," I asked.

"Yes, but the doorway is still *open*." Mr. Green said. He had quite a head for the details. Clearly the Historical Society was lucky to have him, as was I. He was right. The doorway had been lodged open by Manny and the talisman. The talisman was still at the high school and the doorway was...*my house*!

"We have to go!" I yelled. "Father, would you please come with us? We may need your help."

"Of course," Father McLaughlin said, as we all ran to the Ford. The car was battered on all sides and had no headlights.

"To the high school first," Mr. Green said as he got in the driver's seat. I sat up front too. Father McLaughlin opened the rear door and found Manny still lying across the back seat.

"Who's this, then?" Father McLaughlin asked.

"That's my friend Manny," I answered. The Father lifted Manny's head and propped him up against the opposite door. Manny's eyes were closed but he was still breathing. Father McLaughlin closed the door just as Mr. Green put the transmission in drive and hit the gas. We raced back to the high school.

****

While we drove, I explained the story to Father McLaughlin. From a distance, I could see flames as we neared the football field parking lot. This must have been where the police went. A single cruiser was inside the gate near the storage building almost in the exact spot Mr. Topaz had parked earlier. A fire truck was on the football field near the end of the bleachers. No one said anything but I knew that all our hearts sank. The fire engulfed the backhoe and the grass around it, and the backhoe was on its side. Fuel must have poured from the overturned tank, and the fire truck was spraying it down.

Mr. Green stopped along the road without turning in. "We need the talisman from the stone marker so we can close the doorway. If we talk to the police, they'll ask us why we're here. We can't spare the time."

"What about Mr. Topaz?" I asked.

"I can only hope that he's alright and that the police and firemen are helping him right now. But, this will all be for nothing if we don't close that doorway. We have to cut through the trees and try to get that talisman," Mr. Green said.

"It didn't budge the last time we tried," I reminded him.

"Yes, but now that Mr. Black is gone, his control over the talisman should be gone too. At least I hope so," Mr. Green added.

I said no more. I got out of the car and ran off into the darkness along the intersecting road that led to the wooded area. I was almost to the intersection when I veered off into the woods.

I could hear the firemen spraying the flaming backhoe and yelling to each other. I crept along the pathway until the burning machine was in front of me. It cast off quite a bit of light; however, no police or firemen were on my side of the fire. I kept low and sneaked up behind the large stone. The talisman was still there. I crouched down and reached up to it and grabbed it. It came into my hand with ease, and I crept back to the woods and ran.

Soon I was on the street and back inside the battered Ford.

"I have it!" I said, holding it up.

"Excellent. Let's go," Mr. Green said and made a U-turn, heading away from the school.

Once we were away he added, "Could you see anything?"

"No, not from where I was." I answered. We sped towards my house in silence leaving Mr. Topaz and my Dad behind once again.

Chapter 41

*A*s we turned onto my street, I could see a crowd of people by the light of the streetlamps across the street from my house. Mr. Green stopped the car and I got out and raced to the house. I heard him call after me, but I couldn't stop myself from running towards my home.

There was no fire, and lights were everywhere in the house, except it was dark where my bedroom used to be. Now, instead of a wall, there was a huge gaping hole in the side of the house.

"I'm over here," I heard my Mom say behind me. Mom, wrapped in her bathrobe with slippers on her feet, was one of the many people who had congregated across the street. Cadence stood beside her holding little Tony's hand. I ran to them, as Mr. Green got out and went with Father McLaughlin to inspect the house.

"What happened?" I asked.

"I was in the hallway when I saw your friend, Tony, in the living room. He was trying to tell me to get out when I went to him then the house exploded. If he didn't come get me I could've been hurt in the blast," Mom said, her voice cracking. She looked as if she had been crying. I suddenly realized what had really happened. Mr. Black had appeared in the portal which, until then, had been covered by the corner of the house. He burst out and stormed off to find Manny and to find the rest of us. Fortunately, Tony had returned; he saved my mother.

"Where's your father?" Mom asked.

"Dad's still at the high school," I answered her then went to Cadence. I looked around and saw that there was no other damage in the neighborhood.

"Did you find Manny?" Mom asked again.

"Yes, he's in the car asleep," I said pointing to the ruined Ford.

"Is that Father McLaughlin with Mr. Green?"

"Yes, he's here to help."

"What happened to the car?" Cadence asked. Tony was on one side and my Mom on the other; she was holding Tony's hand.

"I'll fill you in later," I said to her and took her hand. "Thanks for staying with my Mom. Did you hear the explosion from your house?"

"No, I just knew to come. I woke up, got dressed and found your Mom outside. We've been standing here ever since."

"Did you call the police or the fire department?" I asked my mother.

"No, Mr. Blanche went inside to do that a little while ago; I haven't seen him since."

Mr. Mason ran up and said, "I talked to the police dispatcher. He said all of the units are tied up with something but they'll have somebody here as soon as possible. I told them that there was no fire and no injuries."

"What could be tying up the police and fire departments at this hour?" Mom asked.

"Well, I heard a lot of commotion on my scanner. There's a fire at the high school by the maintenance building and some wild animal is running amok downtown," Mr. Mason said.

Cadence looked to me with wide eyes. Mom looked concerned as well. "Isn't your father at the high school?" she asked.

"Yes, Mom, but not near the fire."

Mr. Green came up and pulled me aside. "Do you have the stone?" he asked.

Father McLaughlin was behind him.

"Yes, right here," I said and pulled it from my coat pocket. We started for the house and left Father McLaughlin to calm my mother. Cadence and Tony followed.

"Do you know what to do with this?" Mr. Green asked.

"No, I was hoping that you did," I answered. We were at the side of the house that my room was on, the hole was more on the first floor than in my room. It was a large gash in the house, easily wide enough to walk through.

"Just be careful. The house may be structurally unsound on this side now," Mr. Green advised.

I stepped into the laundry room, directly underneath my closet on the floor above.

"I think you'll have to go there and come back to close the doorway," Mr. Green offered. "Cadence, you and your friend should stay over here with me."

"I'll be right back," I said to them. I closed my eyes and concentrated my breathing. I focused on the circle of markers and the Chiefs. I stood there for a while but nothing was happening. I opened my eyes and looked to Cadence, Tony and Mr. Green twenty feet away.

"Nothing is happening," I said.

"Wait there for me," Tony replied. He let go of Cadence and walked towards the hole in the house. Cadence let him go without grievance. Tony carefully picked his way through the shattered wood and joined me. He took my hand and put his head against me.

I began again. I focused my breathing on my midsection and concentrated on the circle of markers. I felt a gentle breeze and wasn't sure if it was from the hole in the house. I opened my eyes and a sunny day brightened before me. Tony and I were back in the circle and all of the Chiefs were with us. They stood at their stones and looked at us from the edge.

The Fire Chief came to us from his position; he was smiling broadly. He stopped in front of me and patted my shoulder. I took the stone from my pocket and offered it to him. He took it from me and placed it in his shoulder bag.

"We cannot stay," I said to him, hoping he would understand me, "We have to get back home."

The Fire Chief did not respond. Instead, he returned to his position on the circle. I looked around at the bright, beautiful day. I smelled the wildflowers and saw the trees sway in the gentle breeze. I almost wanted to stay.

"Take us back now, please," Tony said. He didn't move for the entire brief visit. I didn't answer him; I simply closed my eyes and concentrated my breathing again. I thought of home and my family, my community and my friends. They were all safe, at least for the time being.

Epilogue

We stayed at Grandma's house while the house was inspected and the insurance company worked to get us compensated for the damages. Even though the hole burst outward from the house, our claim was for a lightning strike. Fortunately, no one in the neighborhood had actually seen Mr. Black so it seemed very plausible. The hole was boarded up and the contractor said that there was no structural damage. Our home would be as good as new whenever they got around to fixing it.

Dad had three broken ribs and the doctor said he was very fortunate not to have had his lung punctured. He was in the hospital for a while, and then he came home to convalesce before he returned to work. Manny had come out of his stupor shortly after Cadence and I returned. His parents had thought he'd stayed over the night and had been with us the whole time, so they were none the wiser. Manny was his old self and only remembered enough of the events to be convinced that everything actually happened. He found the crucifix in his pocket that I had placed there and swore that it helped to save him.

Mr. Topaz was not harmed during the battle with Mr. Black. He jumped free from the backhoe as it was teetering towards the fall. Mr. Black was so involved with the machine that he did not notice Mr. Topaz run to the school. There, Mr. Topaz broke a window on the old side of the school that had not been converted to safety glass. He climbed in and pulled the fire alarm; he only had minor cuts and scrapes to show for it.

It was then that Mr. Topaz noticed my Dad's car in the parking lot near the tennis courts. When he looked in he found my Dad in tough shape in the back seat. He hopped into the car and found the keys in the ignition, drove my father to the hospital and waited with him. By then, we and the Ford were gone and Mr. Black was on his way to the church.

When the police and fire departments arrived, they found the backhoe in flames and the lock to the storage building cut. They also found the broken window when they went to silence the alarms. With no one there, they blamed vandals.

The unfortunate officer who had encountered Mr. Black was at a loss when describing him, so he described him as a large animal of some kind. Mr. Black put a few dents in the police cruiser and Officer Brown was disciplined for discharging his weapon without cause. Beyond that, he was more than happy to forget the whole night.

Mr. Green proved to be a very skillful driver as Officer Brown had never actually seen the Ford belonging to Mr. Topaz screaming through the streets of the town. All the damage the car received was from Mr. Black. Other than some downed phone lines, the town escaped without a scratch. The insurance company called the Ford a total loss and provided Mr. Topaz with a check to go buy another one.

Father McLaughlin became a full-fledged member of the town's Historical Society and was entrusted with the secrets within. He not only was witness to some of the events of Memorial Day but assisted in resolving the situation with grace. The next morning, in the light of day, Father McLaughlin went to the statue of St. Mary behind his parish and saw the makeshift grave.

He picked up the shovel I had left behind and neatened the job. That afternoon he purchased plants, some mulch and some decorative garden pieces from Tippy's Garden Center. He used the supplies to landscape the area around St. Mary so that it blended in nicely with the well-manicured lawn of the church. He was mindful enough to make sure that he returned the shovel to Mr. Topaz.

Before all of that, he performed a brief but Catholic burial service behind the statue. He took the rosary beads he had been carrying with him the night before and buried them with the remains of the outcast Namtuxet Chief. Father McLaughlin would tend to that garden for the rest of his days at the Lady of the Rosary. Mr. Black appears to still be resting in peace right to this day.

I still haven't written that letter to Anthony Delmarre's family; I haven't figured out what to say. I kept the little mask hoping that one day I'll have the courage to finally sit down and write.

Manny and I remain best friends. Cadence and I officially became boyfriend and girlfriend. And I finally accepted the idea of myself as a Chief and a Guardian of the Doorway — of *our* Doorway. I was aware there were hundreds of doorways throughout, and for each one of them, were guardians who were likely even more skillful as I was in their roles.

We three young people are the newest members of the Historical Society. The Society keeps our secrets and works closely with us to assure there are no nefarious beings trying to make passage into our world.

With the continued aid provided by my Dad, Father McLaughlin, Mr. Green and Mr. Topaz, we still keep watch over our townspeople and over you.

Acknowledgements

Hello reader! Thank you for taking the time to join me on this little adventure, I hope that you enjoyed it.

This is a work of fiction, I'm sure that you figured that out on your own. The Namtuxet tribe mentioned is also fictional though influenced by the actual Native American tribes that resided (and still reside) in southern New England. As all tribes throughout the country, these are a fascinating people and evidence of their history still surrounds us. Take an opportunity to learn more about them and the history of where you live, you may be surprised at some of the things that happened in your neighborhood, even right where you are standing.

In the *Step Patrick* series, I mention King Philip's War and some of the actual events and places nearby. Though the town of Leighton is also fictional, it is nestled in southeastern Massachusetts where many real events have happened over the course of history. Look for Anawan Rock, Nine Men's Misery, King Philip's Seat or King Philip's Cave just to name a few.

This is the second edition of *Carved In Stone* and I'd like to take this opportunity to thank the many people who helped make it and the whole Step Patrick series possible.

My editor, Pamela Loring (pamelaloring.net), is fabulously talented. Her ability to take this morass of ideas and make it into something polished is undeniable. She is patient, kind and considerate and, hopefully, we will be working together well into the future.

My proofreader, Sheila Laclair, is a blessing; thank you Sheila!

Thanks to my family and friends for riding along on this crazy train and keeping my wheels on the tracks.

Special thanks to author Alan Porter for seeing something special in the original manuscript and encouraging me to follow through.

Thanks to author Robert Hyldburg for his inspiration and friendship.

And thanks to you, my readers, who have surprised me at every turn with kind words and a strong following. I am humbled.

Ken Spears

Kenspearsauthor.webs.com
December 2014

Step Patrick's second thriller, *In Hollow Trees*, is now available at Amazon and other fine retailers!

Step Patrick will return in the third installment - *Mister Midnight.*